Kentucky Home

Kentucky Home

Sarah Title

KENSINGTON BOOKS

http://www.kensingtonbooks.com

KENSINGTON BOOKS are published by

Kensington Publishing Corp.
119 West 40th Street
New York, NY 10018

All Kensington titles, imprints, and distributed lines are available at special quantity discounts for bulk purchases for sales promotion, premiums, fund-raising, educational, or institutional use.

Special book excerpts or customized printings can also be created to fit specific needs. For details, write or phone the office of the Kensington Special Sales Manager: Kensington Publishing Corp., 119 West 40th Street, New York, NY 10018. Attn. Special Sales Department. Phone: 1-800-221-2647.

Kensington and the K logo Reg. U.S. Pat. & TM Off.

eISBN-13: 978-1-60183-114-9
eISBN-10: 1-60183-114-5

First Electronic Edition: June 2013

ISBN-13: 978-1-60183-204-7
ISBN-10: 1-60183-204-4

Printed in the United States of America

To my parents:
Mom, because you always put down your book to listen;
Dad, because this ain't your kind of story,
but you still think it's awesome.

Acknowledgments

Nobody would be reading this book if it weren't for Bobbi Smith and her amazing RT Advanced Writing Workshop. That not only gave me the kick in the pants I needed to finish the book, but she also helped me massage the manuscript into something worth submitting to an editor. She's amazing, and she made me see possibilities I was too chicken to consider myself.

Thank you to my editor (my editor!) Alicia Condon for taking a chance on me. I am still metaphorically sitting on my office floor, trying to take it all in. And to my agent (my agent!!) Louise Fury for some great Hollow Bend jam sessions.

Way back before that, Sarah Glassmeyer and I were riffing on a family-run horse farm and the love it inspires. Our original idea involved sheiks and feisty Irish horse trainers, but the well ain't dry yet. Also, Craig Lefteroff helped me come up with the original name for this book: *Harlequestrian*.

Over the course of several years, I brought pieces of this book to my amazing writing group, the Black Dogs. None of them read romance, but ha, ha, I fooled them. Beverly Delidow (thanks for the toad joke), Jen Grover, Matt Wolfe, Llewellyn McKernan, Jenn Hancock, Carol Brodtick, Marc Miller—thank you for all of your support, feedback, and horse stories. And now you can read the love scenes.

A few people heard tell of my foray into romance writing, and have been cheerleaders and readers and publicists: Toni Blessing, the best boss ever; Tricia Stringer (and our boyfriend, Adam Harris), who reads stealthily but promotes boldly; Pam May, who corrects my Appalachianisms; Marsha Alford and Karan Ireland, who loved this book without even reading it; and Anne McConnell, the secret inspiration for Miss Libby. JK. Also to Emily Bacon, who deserves a Pulitzer for her patient photography in Kanawha State Forest. I do not enjoy having my picture made.

Also to my family, who is insane, but whom I love very much: Tom, Amy, Mary Ellen, and Brian. Thank you all for being psyched for me, even though I didn't tell you forever. Adelaide and Emmett, you guys are too young for this book.

Prologue

Luke Carson sat in a chair on the fire escape outside of his DC apartment window, his feet resting on the railing. He tilted the chair back, breathing in the humid summer night. It wasn't much of a porch, and it wasn't much of a view over the edge of the building next door, but he needed some fresh air. He cracked his beer open and thought it might be time to move on again.

Where to this time? He had a pretty nice gig with this catering company. The hours were flexible, the bartending was easy, and the owner was nice enough to let him share her bed from time to time. She was pretty flexible, too, he thought as he took a long pull of his drink. Still, he itched to move on. Serving watered-down drinks at suburban charity functions was lucrative, especially since his Kentucky charm seemed to help pad the tip jar, but he needed more. The city was starting to stifle him, the long green lawns of DC parks no match for the rolling hills of home.

He laughed. Like he really missed home. Sure, the food was good and the horses were heaven, but going back to his family's farm was like walking on a treadmill set to slow-as-hell. Nothing changed. Nobody took chances, least of all his father. And he'd be damned if he turned into a clone of his father like his brother, Keith, had. Luke couldn't say he blamed Keith for hiding out—some things were too painful to face. But three years . . .

Besides, Luke could think of a lot more appealing places than Hollow Bend, Kentucky to watch opportunities pass him by.

He pulled his phone out of his pocket, checking his missed calls to see if Dave had any word on that breed horse auction. It wasn't exactly on the up-and-up, but it would be good to be part of the excitement.

Three missed calls, all from Mal. What had that girl gotten herself into this time? He hit send to call her back, but hung up when he got her voice mail. He'd see her, eventually, even though she hadn't been at the last few functions he worked at. Not a surprise, considering.

He remembered the first time he'd met her, at a party for the new pediatric wing at a hospital in Maryland. Mal's husband was the man of the hour—apart from the big donors, of course. Michael was the hotshot oncologist, and he made sure everyone knew that it was because of him the wing was being built. He had been courted by the hospital's administration, lauded by the head of the division, blah, blah, blah. Luke listened to the whole thing while waiting to take his drink order.

What Luke had really been looking at, though, was Michael's wife. Luke liked the wives at these things. They were the colorful, curvy plumage that made his job worthwhile. Not the most progressive attitude, but, hey, you can take the boy out of the country . . .

The night he met Mal, she was wearing one of those short, tight numbers the wives favored. Hers was not as short and tight as some, but it was a brilliant blue that made her brown eyes pop, and it was plenty tight that he could tell she was not into starving herself so she was all bones and implants. She was an all-natural woman. All natural, and immune to his charms. Oh, sure, she smiled politely at him, even laughed at one or two of his jokes, but as soon as Michael joined her at the bar, she was all business, introducing Luke to her husband (as if Michael cared), and following him out into the crowd with barely a look back.

Their little dance continued—she'd get her drink, they'd hang out, Michael would commandeer her, and Luke wouldn't see her until the next time. Then he ran into her at a café. Luke was on a date, but when the woman made it clear she wasn't interested (she was Ivy League, he was barely finished high school), he joined Mal, who looked like she needed company. And she was still pretty cute, even without the tight dress.

Over the course of the next month, it became abundantly clear to Luke that Mal didn't need a man on the side. She needed a friend. None of the other hospital wives seemed to care that Michael belittled her in front of them, or that she spent Memorial Day weekend alone because Michael decided that was the only time he could get away from it all to go on a cruise. Who would go on a cruise alone when he had a beautiful woman to go with him?

Luke knew the answer to that, so he took pity and invited Mal over. His roommate, Claire, was attempting an urban barbecue, and Luke was in charge of grilling on their pathetic little fire escape. Mal brought fruit salad and a look of hope he hadn't seen on her before. It suited her. She was going to stay at the house with Michael for now, she told him, but he'd agreed to a separation. Divorce papers would be drawn up after the holiday weekend.

Claire had given him a look—a don't-you-dare-make-a-move-buddy look. So Luke agreed to meet Mal for coffee, and that was it.

Somehow the only part of leaving he would regret was losing Mal's friendship. He liked that Mal leaned on him for support, and he liked how he made her feel. She listened to him, laughed at his stories, and shook her head when he was being a bastard. She understood him, his need to grab a part of something bigger, but not knowing what that was yet. They had that in common.

A bang at the door interrupted his thoughts. His chair fell forward and he spilled some beer on his shirt.

"Dammit, Claire," he mumbled as he climbed through the window. She'd forgotten her keys. Again. "Good thing I'm off tonight or you'd be sleeping in the hallway."

But it wasn't Claire when he opened the door.

"Mal? What happened?" Her eyes were red, and her right cheek was puffy with the start of a bruise.

"Hey, Luke," she said. "Can I come in?"

Chapter 1

"It turns out staring at the screen won't make the figures add up."

Keith turned in his seat and smiled wearily at Miss Libby as she stuck her head in his doorway, followed by a waft of that sweet rose perfume she wore. He should have seen her walking across the yard to the farm hands' bunk he had converted into a small—very small—one-bedroom home with a living room/office of sorts. But his eyes were crossing just trying to focus on the spreadsheets; he didn't think he could focus anywhere else even if he wanted to.

As Libby entered his office, the smell of coffee overpowered the roses, and he gratefully reached out his hands for the mug she handed him. She bent down to give Peanut a scratch behind the ears. Peanut responded by raising his head half off the floor, then flopping over onto his back, his three legs in the air. Miss Libby obliged him with a belly rub.

"How long have you been at it?"

"Feels like just about a month. But I guess since breakfast." A corner of Keith's mouth lifted. Miss Libby came and stood behind him, resting her hand on his shoulder as she looked at the computer screen.

"How'd we do this month?" She blinked mildly at the computer screen. She was just about as good with numbers as any of the Carsons were, which was not at all. "Never mind. How about a break? I know you must be hungry by now . . ."

"I just want to try to sort this out before—"

"Before, before, before. Keith, sweetheart, come to the house and eat dinner."

"I'll get a plate later."

"Who says there will be any left?"

Keith smiled up at her. "You gonna let me go hungry, Libby?"

"I won't, but your brother might. Luke's back."

Great, thought Keith. *What is it this time? What deal did he find that he just could not pass up?* "Must've been nice for you to see him."

"Said he just got homesick for my cooking. But I know he's worried about this place. And you."

"There's nothing to worry about! I'm—"

"I know, I know, you're fine. It's been three years since you lost Vanessa and you've been fine every day since then. Anyway, don't worry about Luke's questions tonight. He's in a state because he hit traffic on the way in. Lives out of town for a few years and the case of road rage on that boy is unbelievable."

Keith gave her a questioning look. "Traffic?" They had traffic in Hollow Bend?

"The Harvest Festival? Happens every fall, although I can see how you might have missed the leaves changing. I don't think you've set foot off the farm since the summer."

Keith looked guiltily toward the barn that held the official office next to the tack room. There was a window, he was pretty sure, but now the low table in front of the window was piled so high with boxes and papers (mostly bills, he thought miserably) that he could only see out if he stood up. Just as well, since the trees on the rolling hills beyond the house were changing from that sweet mixture of yellow and orange to the brutal red that meant fall was well and truly on its way out. He loved that view. He didn't need the distraction. Still, he should get a file cabinet. Add that to the list of things to make time to do to help him get ahead. Where was that list?

Miss Libby patted his shoulder sympathetically. "You work too much, sweetheart."

"I have to."

Miss Libby stroked the back of his head maternally. "I don't want to argue with you, not when there's a celebration goin' on inside."

"What celebration? I thought Luke was home and cranky. Seems like that happens enough for it to pass unremarked."

"Luke's got himself engaged."

Chapter 2

Mal patted the front of her skirt self-consciously. She had decided to leave with just one suitcase—this was just a short trip, a temporary stop to get her head together, so she didn't need her whole wardrobe. Still, this skirt was not right at all. Oh, sure, the cotton floral print hit right below the knee and the flare of the A-line was the most flattering cut for her curvy shape, or so she had read. But a fall nip was in the air and her legs were freezing, and every time the wind blew, it seemed determined to feel her up. She pulled at the hem of her green T-shirt, then pulled her pink cardigan tight across her chest. She felt like a watermelon. A flowery, freezing watermelon.

"Don't worry, darlin', you look fine." Luke put his arm around her waist and pecked her cheek. He might not be her type, but he sure was warm. She looked up at him, his green eyes shining with laughter.

Mal hated meeting new people. Not that she didn't like people, most people, anyway, but the first meetings were always the worst. Since she was a child she had been told that she did not give a good first impression. When she got nervous, she either ran her mouth off, sounding like an idiot or offending someone's deep-held personal beliefs, or she froze and came across as a stuck-up bitch. That was how Michael described their first meeting. "Never could unfreeze you," he used to say.

Well, she was definitely still freezing.

She had never been to Kentucky before, and she was totally unprepared for how beautiful it was. Luke insisted that Hollow Bend was a nothing town in the middle of nowhere; and in Kentucky, that's twice as nowhere as anywhere else in the country. It took them almost ten hours to drive from DC. As they got closer to the Kentucky border, Mal began to think that they would pull off the interstate into a trailer park where she would be greeted by his cousin and his cousin's wife, also his cousin. The interstate was beautiful—well, the interstate was pretty normal-looking asphalt, but it was surrounded by rolling green hills and those iconic white horse fences that she thought people just made up to put in scenic calendars.

Luke was right, though. Hollow Bend was in the middle of nowhere. When they pulled off the interstate, they drove about half an hour on a road that went from four lanes to two, then down to one across a bridge over a river that actually babbled. She knew they were in town, not just because of the line of shabby storefronts, but because there were other cars on the road. Luke kept punching the steering wheel, complaining about heavy traffic. Having lived in the DC suburbs for years, Mal didn't think she would ever refer to a dozen pickup trucks as heavy traffic, but Luke did, so she thought she'd do her best to fit in. Damn country drivers, don't know how to read a stop sign.

The Carsons lived twenty minutes out of town (on the outskirts of the middle of nowhere, maybe), down a bumpy road that didn't have a name and that Luke assured her was easier to drive when it was dirt rather than mud. She saw the barn first, a long red one surrounded by those white fences. Horses grazed the fields closer to the road.

"You have horses?"

"This is Kentucky. Everyone has horses. Anyway, most of these aren't ours, we just board them. We have one of those romantic failing family horse farms. It's called Tara."

"It's called what?"

"Tara. The house from *Gone with the Wind*? You really are a Yankee, aren't you?"

"Even I know that's Georgia."

"Hmm. Pretty smart for a Yankee."

They drove past a small sign attached to the fence: WILD ROSE FARM AND STABLES.

"Wild Rose?"

"For my mom," Luke said. He had mentioned that she'd died from breast cancer when he was pretty young. "My dad bought it for her when they got married."

"He bought her a horse farm? Wow."

"Well, he bought the land. They built the house. Is that just a Kentucky thing? Having land is a big deal."

When Mal got married, they moved into a big shiny new house in a gated community. There was a yard, but she had never worked in it. Maybe the land was a Kentucky thing, after all.

"Don't get all dreamy, Mal. It's not as romantic as all that, at least not anymore. It's crumbling and nearly bankrupt."

Mal gazed out the window as they bumped past the horses, coats shining, looking up at the noise of the car and shaking their manes. "I've never been on a horse," she whispered.

Luke's father's house did look like a romantic, crumbling farm house. The black shutters were a little dull, and the yard was more mud than grass. But it was a beautiful house, small but sturdy, with a big wraparound porch that had a weather-beaten wooden rocker and a porch swing. There were lace curtains in all the windows and flowering bushes on either side of the walkway—wild roses, perhaps. From the porch, she could see a smaller, plain house behind the barn, and just as red. The air smelled like there was a fireplace roaring somewhere inside. The whole thing looked like a postcard, cozy and welcoming and warm.

It was not, unfortunately, warm. Miss Libby—call her Libby, she said—met them at the door, bustling and blinking back tears, hustling them inside before they caught their death. Then she bustled off to the kitchen, chasing after a dinging timer and admonishing Luke to make Mal feel at home. Libby was really fast for such a tiny, wide woman.

Mal wished she had listened to Luke and kept her jeans on as she tried to back closer to the fireplace without losing her grip on Luke's arm. She fingered the cheap metal ring she wore. It definitely wasn't gold, although this one wasn't turning her finger green like the one they got out of the vending machine. Still, there was no way anyone would think it was real.

"I don't know about this. I don't want to impose on your family. I don't know them, I can't—"

"Hush. I told you it'd be fine. They would do anything for the woman I love."

"Can't we just say I'm a friend who needs a place to stay?"

"Now what fun would the truth be? Anyway, this will make it easier for them to get to know you, and once they do, they'll love you and do anything for you purely on your own merits and not because you tried to tame the wild beast that is Luke Carson."

As he said the last, he puffed out his chest and squeezed her tighter. She laughed up into his green eyes. Luke had always been able to do that, ever since he tried to pick her up at that fund-raiser in Bethesda almost a year ago. He teased her, but that laugh in his eyes always made her feel, well, comfortable. Good thing she had had her fill of charming, handsome men. Otherwise, she would be in big trouble.

Suddenly a fiery blond streak came charging through the living room and launched itself into his arms. Mal was almost knocked over by the force, but then she found herself clutched into the embrace as well.

"Whoa! Mal, meet my little sister, Katie."

"Luke, you jerk! What is this about you bringing home a fiancée?" The blonde turned to Mal. "Hi there. I don't know how you put up with an animal like my brother, but I love you for it. And if you hurt him, I'll break your legs."

Kate—Katie—was as tall as Luke, maybe an inch taller, and she was long and lean. Mal was pretty sure she was heavier than Katie, but she decided that when the time came for the real story to come out, she was going to be far away from this one. Preferably in a different state. "Hi, I'm Mal." She shook Katie's outstretched hand.

"A firm handshake, I like it. OK, enough nicey-nice, let's eat."

Katie led them into the dining room, which was much more formal than Mal was expecting from the country-comforting interior she saw, not to mention the downright rundown state of the outside of the house. The table sat six, and over a gleaming dark wood tabletop was a brocade table runner in fall hues of red, orange, and green.

Apparently Mal was not the only one impressed. Luke let out a whistle. "Miss Libby went all out. What are those, napkin rings?"

Luke reached for her hand and guided her to a seat next to his. She was grateful for the comfort and she didn't let it go, not even when he tried to pull the chair out for her. "Sorry," she murmured when she realized what she was doing.

"You're OK, baby," he said, and pecked her on the cheek. Mal blushed, not sure how such public displays of affection would go over in this formal setting. Well, formal except for the fact that Mal was the only one not wearing jeans.

She looked up as a chair scraped across the hardwood floor. A tall, imposing man stood and nodded at her. She could definitely see him in Luke—the slope of the nose, the high cheekbones, the green of the eyes. But where Luke had laughter in his eyes, this man revealed nothing but weariness, and maybe a little boredom, like this was nothing he had not seen before. How many women had Luke brought home?

"Dad, this is Mallory, my fiancée. Mal, this is my father, Cal."

He nodded, then nodded at her seat, indicating she should sit. Luke leaned to her ear and said, "What did I tell you, nothing to it."

Mal smiled meekly at Cal, then studiously admired the details on the napkin ring.

Just as she was about to make an insightful comment on making crafts by hand versus machine, which she was sure the horse farmer and the charming bartender would be really interested in, the door to the kitchen swung open and Libby's ample bottom came through.

"Oh, Mallory! Mal, right? OK, let me put down this ridiculous platter and give you another hug." Cal stood to take the plate from her and placed it in front of himself, at the head of the table. Before Mal could say anything, before she could really even stand properly, she was enveloped in strong, soft arms, her back rubbed in that maternal way that brought tears to the eyes of people who didn't get enough mothering. She blinked hard.

"Hi," she said into the shoulder, inhaling some old-lady rose perfume that went completely against the vivaciousness of the woman holding her. "I've heard so much about you."

Miss Libby pulled back, blushing, and cupped Mal's cheeks in her hands. "Well, don't believe a word of it. We're thrilled to have you here. You must be one special gal to have tamed this wild one." She reached over one hand and patted Luke's cheek. One hand on each of their cheeks, she looked at Mal, then at Luke, then back again. "Aren't you two just the sweetest—" Libby's eyes misted over. Mal looked to Luke for help, which was not forthcoming. "Luke, if your mother could see you . . ."

"That's enough," Cal practically barked from his place at the head of the table. "Let's eat."

"All right, all right. Katie, come help me bring out the rest of the food."

"Can I help with anything?" Mal asked.

Katie laughed. "No, dearie," she said in a pretty good imitation of Miss Libby's voice, "you're the guest of honor and you won't lift a finger. Whereas Katie could use a few lessons in being a proper lady so she'll bow and scrape and serve the men like all good women of the twenty-first century ought to."

Katie let out a very unladylike snort, but followed Libby through the swinging doors. Mal meticulously unrolled her napkin from the ring and spread it over her lap.

"So, Mr. Carson, I saw that you have horses here?"

Cal looked up at her, then at Luke, his eyes narrowing a little. "Call me Cal," he said to her.

When he didn't offer anything else, Mal continued, "I was telling Luke that this is my first time in Kentucky, and I can't believe how beautiful it is. This house is amazing. How old is it? It looks like it's at least a hundred years old, but Luke said you built it? I love old houses, I feel like there are so many stories inside . . ." She trailed off when she realized Cal was staring at her.

"Your girl sure talks a lot," he said to Luke. Great first impression, Mal.

She turned her head and said meekly to Luke, "Sorry."

"Don't worry about it, baby, ol' Cal here must've just left his manners in the barn."

"Buried under the shit you should be helping me muck out."

Well. That was something, a nice pre-dinner guilt trip. Mal was about to cut the tension with several comments about how little she knew about horses, when the kitchen door swung open again, but it wasn't Katie or Libby. It was all Mal could do to stifle a gasp. He was a big guy, a real-man kind of man. The kind who split wood for fun, or whatever people in the country do to show how strong they are. His strength radiated from under his plaid flannel shirt, sleeves rolled up to reveal powerful forearms. His jeans were well worn, distressed from use, not from the factory. His brown hair was darker than Luke's, and shaggier, like he needed a haircut. It suited him. Mal blinked, shocked by his careless, unconscious manliness.

Of course, nothing was manlier than the set of floral potholder mitts he was using to carry a steaming bowl of potatoes.

He put the bowl down on an empty trivet and nodded to Luke. Was Luke the only man in this family who spoke?

"Keith, this is my fiancée, Mal. Mal, my older brother, Keith."

Huh. Luke hadn't mentioned having a brother. But there was no mistaking the family resemblance. The lines around his bright green eyes matched Luke's, from too much sun or too much laughter. No, Mal thought, not too much laughter. His eyes were like Cal's, a little tired and a little sad.

"Hi." She stood up and reached out a hand to him. He extended his hand to her, then retracted it fast, pulling the oven mitt off. His gaze locked on hers, searching, maybe a little suspicious. She broke the handshake first, pulling her hand away a little fast, and swinging wide to indicate how nice the house was (true), how welcome she felt here (lie), and a million other things she had to say to counter the stifling silence of these big men. In her enthusiasm, though, she knocked her hand into one of the candlesticks. Before it could even finish its wobble, Keith grabbed the base and set it right. She looked at him, blushing, starting to come up with the words to express how much she would regret burning down such a nice house, especially on her first day there.

"Nice to meet you."

Then he turned on his heel and walked back into the kitchen.

Chapter 3

Mal looked around the tiny bedroom she'd been, as Luke said, assigned. The plaid bedspread was more shabby than chic, but it looked warm and she was desperate to climb under the covers. She had started changing when she realized that she had nothing appropriate to change into—in addition to no dressy fall weather clothes, she also had no pajamas. Katie was going to lend her some sweats to sleep in, although Mal was dubious about how far over her hips they would go. Katie was tall, but she was thin as a reed. And she still managed to look like a pipsqueak next to her brothers. No wonder Luke was so protective. At one time, that would have driven her crazy. Now Mal was grateful for the protective interference of Luke Carson.

He had told her that was what the men in his family did, looked out for the women. Mal thought that was a pretty unenlightened attitude, but she was in no position to turn it down. She had known Luke for less than a year, and even though their friendship had been slow to develop—he was just the charming bartender she sometimes saw at charity events when she was on Michael's arm—now she didn't know what she would do without him. She knew he had a wild, restless streak, and he was getting ready to leave DC anyway. But for him to pick up and come *home*, a home he only talked about as a punch line, a place she knew he did not feel, well, at home, that was big, and it was all for her. She had no one else—no family, no real friends beyond Luke. But he made her feel like this was the easiest, most natural thing in the world, to put a fake ring on a friend's finger and take her home.

She had a hard time imagining the other men in the Carson family being as sweet about it. Probably as high-handed (and Luke was high-handed—she was here, wasn't she? And without any pajamas?). There was nothing sweet about Cal and Keith Carson, although Mal had to admit that Keith didn't have the same hardness that Cal did. Maybe that would come with time. For now, Keith seemed happy to wear floral oven mitts and hold out Libby's chair for her. Oh, manners. Manners were very sexy. Maybe he had a mommy complex, she thought, fingering the fraying corner of the comforter. She shook her head. This was Kentucky, not *Oedipus*.

Besides, she was engaged to Luke. So even if she did find her gaze lingering on Keith's sad eyes or his strong forearms, it didn't matter. She was here for however much time it took Michael to forget about her, and for her to make a plan for what she was going to do for the rest of her life.

No big deal.

A knock at the door interrupted her thoughts. Luke snuck in before she could answer. "Luke! You're not supposed to be in here!"

"Can't I sneak in to say good night to my best girl?"

She didn't really mind, and if they really were engaged, she would have welcomed it. But Miss Libby had told her that she knew it was old-fashioned, but in this house, two people did not share a bed unless they were married. She said it with a smile, which seemed to be the only way Miss Libby said anything. But still.

Luke came over to put his arms around her, but she pushed at his chest. "Luke, get out. I don't want to face the wrath of Miss Libby if we get caught."

"Miss Libby won't care. She likes you, she told me."

"She likes me until she catches me taking your virtue under her roof when she expressly said it was forbidden."

"Darlin', if I ever had virtue, it was gone a long time ago."

"Well, then if she catches you taking my virtue."

Luke just raised an eyebrow at her. "Katie gave me these for you."

He handed her a pair of sweatpants and a very old, ratty-looking T-shirt. At least it looked big. She immediately started to slip the sweats on under her skirt. Ah, warmth. She sighed to herself.

"Come here, sit down," Luke said, indicating the bed. It was her turn to raise an eyebrow at him. "I'm not going to do anything un-virtuous. I just want to talk to you." When she sat, he said, "How are you doing?" and started rubbing her shoulders.

She moaned, letting her head roll forward. "Fine. A little awkward. I know you insist I'm not, but I still feel like I'm imposing."

Luke tsked at her and rubbed up her neck to the bottom of her skull.

It took a Herculean effort to turn and take his hands in hers. "Luke, please be serious. I can find another—"

"Mal, we're in the middle of nowhere—"

"But if Michael—"

"And we're country people. We have guns." He smiled and gently stroked the skin under her right eye where the bruise had faded to nothing. "You just needed to lay low for a while. Well, you ain't gonna find anyplace lower than Hollow Bend," he said, his Kentucky accent exaggerated. When she started to protest, he reached up and grasped her chin between his thumb and forefinger. "Trust me. You're safe here. You can take all the time you need."

Her eyes moistened, and she shivered. Not from cold, really—although a little from the cold.

Luke noticed. "Sweetheart, you're freezing. Get under here." He pulled the covers back while she quickly changed her shirt and pulled off her skirt. She crawled under the covers, and Luke kicked off his shoes and climbed in with her.

"Luke—" she started to protest.

"I'm not going to touch your virtue. I'm just getting you warm is all. Damn, girl, you're an icicle." His arms wrapped around her; his hands pulled her head to his chest. "Just relax, try to get some sleep. I reckon you haven't had a good night's sleep in a while."

That was true enough. Before she could only lie stiffly next to Michael, hoping not to alert him to her presence in case she woke him in the middle of the night. There were two possible Michaels who could wake up—the cranky Michael who complained that she was preventing him from getting the sleep he needed to be able to perform in the operating room, or the amorous Michael, who was just as unpleasant. The one time she snuck out of bed to sleep on the couch was a very unpleasant morning for her. "How would it look," he said, "if people knew they weren't even sleeping in the same bed?" How would they know? she thought, but she never did it again, even after they were separated. Well, at least when he slept at home.

Nothing at all like beautiful Luke, with his sparkling green eyes and his mess of wavy blond hair, his happy-go-lucky attitude that drew people to him, his sweet, sweet heart that wanted to keep her safe. She loved him. She wasn't sure if she would ever be able to fall in love again, not the way she had been with Michael in the beginning, but she did love Luke. She leaned forward and tentatively placed her lips on his. She felt him flinch in surprise, then warm to the idea as her lips moved over his. He put his hand on her shoulder and gently pushed her back.

"Sweetheart, what are you doing?" he said, cupping her cheek in his hand.

"Just testing. Seeing how it felt. You know, if it still felt the same."

"How did it feel?"

Mal sighed. "Like friends."

Luke's laughing eyes met hers. "And how are we going to stay friends if you keep trying to seduce me every time you feel a little low? That's not good for my self-esteem, darlin'."

Now Luke stroked her hair and whispered to her to trust him, that she was safe, that he would take care of her.

She fell asleep.

Mal turned the dark corner, running toward the light at the end of the hallway. She wasn't sure where she was or where she was going, but she heard footsteps behind her and she knew she had to get ahead of them. She ran and ran, her legs pumping, muscles burning, and when she got to the light, her momentum propelled her through the doorway out into empty space. There was no floor beyond the doorway and she was falling . . .

She woke up with a gasp and shot straight up in bed. Where was she? Plaid quilt—hotel room? Slowly the details started to take shape in her sleep-addled brain. Football trophies on the walls. Worn wooden floors. Luke's house. Well, Luke's family's house. Luke had murmured her to sleep. She turned around in the bed; she blearily scanned the room.

Luke was gone.

Chapter 4

Keith was up with the roosters the next morning. Since his dad got up that early, he knew Miss Libby would have some breakfast out. No one was in the kitchen when he crossed the yard and went in through the back door, so he wrapped a couple of pieces of bacon in a paper towel and stuffed a biscuit in his mouth. He turned back to stuff another biscuit in his pocket, then headed out to the bunkhouse.

His little house wasn't much to look at, but it was sturdy. The outside needed painting, something he should have done this summer but never got around to. He made a mental note to corral Luke into helping him while he was home. For however long he was home. He noticed Luke's car was gone from the driveway, but he didn't think anything of it. Luke kept the most irregular hours of any man he had ever met. He knew Miss Libby hoped that fiancée of his would straighten him out; didn't seem to be working so far.

Mal. She seemed nice enough. OK, she seemed downright sweet. Not that phony kind of sweet he was used to seeing around town, girls who would bat their eyes and laugh at your jokes until they found out that, no, his no-good brother was not in town and, no, he still was not over his dead wife. At least they were natural blondes, which was something Mal definitely was not. He didn't pretend to know about the ins and outs of women's hair coloring, but when Vanessa dyed her hair ("Frosted," she corrected in his head), it looked different, but good. Brought out the blue in her eyes. Mal's hair seemed to make her look a little sick. He felt bad for Luke when he broke the bad news to her that there were no hair salons in Hollow Bend, although maybe Jack would be visiting his horse again soon.

He was still a hairdresser, right? Keith should store that away to tell Mal. She looked high maintenance.

Why the hell would Keith be telling her when the hairdresser was coming to town? Probably because of the way her brown eyes shone when she looked at Luke. Keith was ashamed to admit he was a little jealous. Of course, her eyes shone when she looked at the spread at dinner, too, much to Miss Libby's delight. Mal said she hadn't had a home-cooked meal in years. So much for a domestic goddess to straighten Luke out. Well, hopefully she would at least be able to keep up with him.

He opened the side door of the house and was greeted with much tail wagging and barking. Peanut jumped up, almost knocking Keith over with his one front paw as he made a grab for the bacon in Keith's left hand. Keith pushed him down with a stern, "No." Peanut looked chagrined, and gazed hopefully at the biscuit Keith unwrapped. "Dog, when are you gonna learn?" He laughed this time as Peanut jumped up to snag the crumb Keith threw him. Peanut might have only three legs, but he acted like a four-legged dog. A four-legged lapdog puppy, really. Keith would have been more amused if the ninety pounds of self-deluded canine hadn't just knocked him over, grabbed the bacon out of his hand, and run toward the house.

Mal was having the weirdest dream. She was a kid, running through the sprinklers at her parents' house in Connecticut, when Michael pulled up in his black convertible and honked the horn. Suddenly she was a teenager, home from college for the summer, running out to meet him in cutoffs and flip-flops. Michael looked her up and down, then reached under the seat and pulled out a pistol and shot her—but it was a water pistol, and she got soaked. He got out of the car and soaked her and soaked her, knocking her down and sitting on her chest, soaking her and licking her face, and he had the most terrible morning breath . . .

Mal opened her eyes and looked at the giant furry face on top of hers only to get a lick in the eye. As her thoughts came into focus, she realized what the heavy weight on her chest was—a giant licking shag rug with terrible morning breath.

* * *

Keith ran through the open kitchen door whose screen was now sporting an impromptu doggy hatch. How far could Peanut have gone on three damn legs? He ran through the first floor and was just headed up the stairs when he heard a blood-curdling scream. Mal.

He bolted up the stairs into Mal's room and saw her cowering in the corner of her bed, her legs bent in front of her to fend off Peanut's aggressive friendliness. She was clearly terrified. "Peanut, come!" he shouted. Peanut turned and looked at Keith, gave Mal one last lick on the nose, and ran to Keith.

Katie had come up behind him, rumpled and bleary-eyed. "What the hell is going on?"

"Take Peanut downstairs."

"Hey, Mal, are you OK? You look a little green."

Mal was frozen in her defensive position on the bed.

"Take the dog out, Kate."

Katie turned and obeyed Keith, Peanut limping happily as she led him by the collar. Keith turned to Mal and approached her gently. "Mal? Can you hear me?" She stared blankly at the doorway even though he was fully in the room. She was in a full-blown panic. "Mal, it was a dog. His name is Peanut. He's gone now; Katie took him outside. Mal, the dog is gone."

She turned slowly and looked up at him and whispered, "I think I'm going to throw up now."

She should have been embarrassed that her fiancé's brother was witnessing her morning breath, ill-fitting sweats, and paralyzing fear of dogs, but all Mal knew was that if she didn't get to the bathroom soon, she would have something much grosser to be embarrassed about. Last night's dinner roiled in her stomach, fighting with the aftereffects of her panic. She looked up to Keith, begging for help like he'd helped save her from the dog. "I think I'm going to throw up now."

Before she knew what was happening, she was gently lifted off the bed and carried into the bathroom. Keith set her down on the rug, lifted the toilet seat, and . . . did not turn away in horror as she retched into the bowl. Instead, he got a glass of water from the sink, then kneeled down next to her, rubbing her back and holding her hair out of the way.

Wasn't that one of the tests to see if your man was worthwhile?
Didn't she read that in *Cosmo*? Throw up in front of him, and if he
runs away, it was never meant to be, but if he holds your hair and
rubs your back, he's yours to keep? Unfortunately, this one was not
hers in the first place, but damn, his hands were comforting, warm
on her cold neck, gently kneading the tension out of her shoulders.

"I'm sorry about the dog. Peanut hasn't come to terms with his
size just yet."

"S'okay. It's a farm," Mal answered weakly.

"Still. I shouldn't bring my work home."

Mal blinked up at him for a second. "That huge thing is named
Peanut?"

"Well, yeah," Keith said self-consciously. "He was little when we
found him."

Mal smiled wanly and reached for her toothbrush. "Sorry for
freaking out just there."

"No, don't apologize, it's not—I mean, I should have been more
careful."

Mal tried to talk while brushing her teeth. "Mmmm-hmm-
mmmm-mm-mm-mmm."

Keith looked at her patiently. She spit into the sink. She was still
shaky, but the mint of the toothpaste tasted good. "I don't usually
get sick. Usually I just stand there paralyzed while people tell me
how nice their dog is."

"Well, I've seen how serious fear of animals can be, even if it
seems unwarranted."

"I just, well, ah, I don't know. I've just been afraid for as long as
I can remember. When I was a kid, my neighbor had a really old
mutt. He was mean, but I was little so I tried to pet him. He bit my
chin." She pointed to a miniscule scar on the edge of her chin. "It
scared me, and it hurt. And, obviously, I'm scarred for life." She
managed a weak laugh.

"Shh, it's OK," Keith said, rubbing his hands up and down her
arms. They were covered in goose bumps, and she realized that she
had begun shivering as she told the story.

"Peanut really is a very nice dog. One day, when you're ready, you
can meet him properly. See if you guys get along."

She turned around and looked at Keith, this sweet, sexy man who held her hair when she threw up and didn't laugh at her fear of dogs. "Thank you," she said, and took his hand.

That's where Miss Libby found them as she climbed up the stairs with a mug of tea. "You poor thing," she said, elbowing Keith out of the way and handing the mug to Mal. "Drink this; it'll settle your stomach." She put a protective arm around Mal's waist and led her back into the bedroom.

"See you," Keith practically grunted as he brushed past them in the bathroom doorway.

"That boy and his dog," Miss Libby said, watching him go.

Mal smiled, then laughed, and put her head down. Miss Libby brought her arms up and began to rock back and forth, rubbing Mal's back. It felt good and comforting, but not nearly as good as Keith's arms had, her voice not nearly as soothing as Keith's. Mal's laughter suddenly choked her and turned into tears.

"Whoa, whoa, hey, none of that," said Miss Libby, lifting her chin up and wiping her tears with her thumb. "What's this about?"

Mal tried to explain; she wasn't entirely sure herself. Every time she tried to articulate why she was crying, it just got worse. She didn't like lying and it was stressing her out, she was angry that she was such a chicken around dogs, she was sad that she couldn't have a normal fiancé whose family would take her in because they were engaged for real, but mostly she was frustrated that while she was engaged to one handsome Carson brother, she was thinking about another one entirely.

She decided to keep that last part to herself.

Maybe all of it, but especially that last part.

"I'm sorry. I'm causing such a fuss."

"None of that," Miss Libby clucked. "It's nice to have someone new to fuss over. It's my bread and butter, sweetie. Besides, you make me feel appreciated." She smiled. "Now, I have some bad news about Luke," Miss Libby said kindly.

Mal's eyes widened in panic. "What happened to Luke? Is he OK?"

"Oh, he's fine. But did you know that I don't sleep well? I have a tendency to putter around the house in the middle of the night." Mal nodded, not understanding. "So I saw him leave your room at three o'clock this morning."

Mal blushed.

"That's right, you should look chagrined. But Luke told me nothing untoward happened, and I believe him. Not that it would do much good. Anyway, he told me he had to leave town for a few days."

"What? Why?"

"You might as well get used to it if you're not already. That boy cannot sit still. He's always out, chasing his next big thing. He told me he had a few things to take care of and he'll be back in a few days, and in the meantime, I'm to take good care of you." She pulled a piece of notebook paper out of her robe pocket. "And he gave me this for you."

Mal——

   I know you'll be surprised to wake up alone, but don't worry. I have a big opportunity I have to follow up on or it will fall through. Wipe that worried look off your face; it has nothing to do with Michael. You're fine with my family and I'll be back soon. I love you, darlin', even if it's not that way.

                                        Luke

"Did you read this?" she asked Miss Libby.

"Is it addressed to me?" she responded. Mal looked down at the note, her eyes watering. "Oh, now don't you start that again. He'll be back. He wouldn't have left you here with us if he wasn't coming back."

"Just residual effects of the shock, I guess," Mal lied, wiping her eyes. "And the kindness."

Miss Libby looked like she didn't believe her for a second, but she took her hand. "I am sorry for the shock, and we'll see what we can do about keeping that dog out of here——"

"Oh, no, don't do anything to Peanut on my account. I'm just a guest. And Keith really likes that dog, I don't want to cause any trouble."

"If you saw the mess that Peanut left on my floors, you would know that your trouble is nothing compared to his. But all right, I'll let him off the hook. But, sweetheart, you're going to have to get used to it."

"The dog?"

"The kindness."

Chapter 5

Mal walked out the kitchen door and stood on the step for a second, inhaling the crisp fall air deeply. She buttoned her new corduroy jacket and wrapped the thin plaid scarf around her neck. It felt warmer than it had yesterday; of course, today she was wearing jeans. The sun was bright and the hills were green and so, OK, her fake fiancé had abandoned her for unknown but, according to Libby, not unexpected reasons—but there were horses. She smiled to herself as she crossed the yard toward the fenced-in enclosure where several horses were grazing. They snorted and flicked their ears as she approached. Was it bad to feed horses? Did they bite? What did horses eat?

They were chewing on the short grass near the fence, one of them trying to stick its snout underneath to try to reach the taller grass on the other side. Mal pulled a handful up and leaned her arm over the fence. "Come here, boy! Here's some delicious grass for you. Please don't bite my hand off." The horse sniffed, blowing a warm wet breath onto her hand, then opened its lips to take the grass from her.

"Whoa, you have really big teeth. I mean, you're very beautiful and powerful. And thank you for not biting me." She stood on the bottom rung of the fence to lean over and pet the horse's back. His hair was coarser than she expected, but it was smooth, almost like skin. "You're a strong one, aren't you? I bet you get all the ladies."

"That's actually a female horse."

Mal started, standing up and pulling her hand back, nearly falling off the fence in the process. Keith stood on the other side of the fence, holding a beat-up-looking tin bucket, which he placed in front of the horse, who began to drink.

"How can you tell?" Mal asked. Then, blushing stupidly, said, "Oh. Duh. I didn't think to, um, check."

Keith pushed his cap back and scratched his forehead. He wore scuffed-up boots, one of those quilt-lined plaid shirts, and jeans that looked like they would hold the shape of his hips even after he took them off. He looked sort of deliciously rugged. Like he could be Mr. October in a Handsome Farm Guy Calendar for Women Who Liked Their Dirty Calendars Modest. And Scowling. He was definitely scowling at her.

"OK, well, I didn't come out here to molest the horses. Just, you know, looking around." He didn't say anything, but continued to look at her. She held on to the top rail of the fence and looked around in what she hoped—really hoped—was a cool and casual assessment of her surroundings. "Very nice. Very horse farmy."

"Did you need something, Mal?"

Just a new life, that's it, thanks. "No, I just thought I'd come out here, see if you need any help or anything."

"You know anything about horses?"

"Well, no."

"How were you planning on helping?"

"I don't know; don't you need slop hauled or something?"

"This isn't a pig farm. We don't have slop."

She was beginning to think he wasn't being charmingly teasing, the way Luke was with her. That he was maybe being sort of a jerk.

She should just turn her back on him, leave him standing there glowering in the morning sun with his stupid jeans and his stupid butt and his stupid rugged good looks. But she had nowhere else to go, nothing else to do. Luke was gone, Libby was too polite to say that she had too much work to do to entertain her, and she didn't even have a good book to read.

"Listen, Mal, I've got too much work to do to entertain you." Apparently he wasn't too polite.

"I'm not asking to be entertained, Keith." She practically spat his name. Man, this guy pissed her off. "I'm just trying to be helpful. I know I don't know what I'm doing, but surely there's some mindless physical task you can give me that will make me tired enough that I don't go crazy sitting on my hands waiting for Luke to come back, since that is all anyone seems to expect me to do."

She had worked herself up into quite a lather. Her knuckles were white on the fence rail, and she was breathing hard.

"Maybe Libby needs help in the kitchen."

"Libby sent me out here. To enjoy myself." She clutched the fence post a little harder.

"Where's Katie?"

"She's out riding."

"Maybe you can go shopping or something."

"I hate shopping. Look, it's not that I'm not grateful for your family's hospitality, because I am. Really. But I have a lot of nervous energy at the moment and, frankly, if you don't give me something to do right now, I'm just going to follow you around until you do."

"I don't really have anything for you to do," Keith said, feeling very nervous. He really didn't want her following him around. She was starting to look a little cute to him.

"Well, what were you about to do?"

"Muck out the stalls, exercise the horses a bit."

"Oh, mucking out the stalls, I've seen that in movies. That's just, like, with a shovel or something, right? I can do that. Then you can exercise the horses and you'll have extra time to stand in the corner and give me scowling looks before dinner."

Keith looked at her, considering. She was flushed with her barely controlled anger and her hair had come loose from her ponytail. As a strand blew across her forehead, she brushed it back, losing her balance on the fence post and landing on her feet, ungracefully, on the ground. Dammit, she was cute.

"I'll show you how to muck out the stalls."

Chapter 6

Stall-mucking smelled a lot worse than Mal thought it would. She thought it was maybe just shoveling out the old hay and sweeping up the dirt and putting down some more hay. Somehow it hadn't quite occurred to her that a horse's stall was also its bathroom.

"I guess you can't just let them out every time they have to go," she mused as Keith handed her a heavy pitchfork.

He just sort of looked at her, his eyebrows raised, and handed her a pair of dirty work gloves. "You sure you don't want to change your pants?"

"No, they're just jeans. They can get dirty." And she had no other pants to change into. She was already feeling large and unwieldy in Luke's old rubber boots because Katie's were too small. Besides, the boots came almost up to her knees——how deep was she going to be mucking?

Keith sighed and lined up the shovel, the broom, and pushed the wheelbarrow to the entrance of the first stall. He walked to the end of the barn and grabbed a hay bale, lifting it by two invisible pieces of twine, his back straining. Jeez, he was strong.

"So," he said, dropping the bale at her feet, "you're just gonna put the dirty straw in here"——he indicated the rusty green wheelbarrow—— "then spread out some new clean straw. Call me when you're done, I'll move the load to the manure pile."

"I think I can move a wheelbarrow. It's not like driving a stick shift."

Keith considered her for a moment; obviously, he was not impressed by her physical strength. "OK, just don't fill it. These things are hard to steer when they're full." He kicked the wheelbarrow like an old man kicks the tires of a car, showing off, testing it out.

The wheelbarrow fell over.

She thought maybe Keith was blushing a little as he bent to set it to rights. Man, he looked good in those jeans. She shook her head. Focus on the manure pile.

"Thanks," she said, thinking about poop. "You want me to do all of these?" The barn seemed to reach to West Virginia, millions of stalls with millions of gallons of excrement needing mucking. Really, she thought as she quickly counted, there were only twenty.

"No, we've only got six horses at the moment. Just do the ones with straw in them."

"Why do you have such a big barn if you've only got six horses?"

"Well, I guess because people prefer to board their horses with the fancy new outfit up the road and don't want to deal with a socially inept old man who won't go out and drum up new business. And because that same old man won't invest in new horses for breeding or for training and won't try any new damn thing, so we have a big old barn with six horses. But that's fewer stalls for you to muck, so don't worry about it."

If this was how Keith was talkative, she wasn't sure she didn't like him better silent.

"Well, thanks for the rant. I'm going to go shovel some poop now." She turned to the first stall.

"Sorry, that wasn't—"

She turned back, eyebrows raised expectantly. He just sort of stared at her, mouth gaping, lost for words, then adjusted his hat and turned.

"Yell if you need a hand," he called over his shoulder, not looking back.

Like she would voluntarily spend more time with him, she thought as she maneuvered the first forkful of dirty straw into the wheelbarrow. The man had the social skills of a barrel. Well, until he started talking. Then he was more like . . . she paused, leaning on her pitchfork. He was a little like Michael. Taking his beef with other people out on her. That made her mad. So she took it out on the horse poop.

* * *

Mal shook the straw out over the last stall, making sure it was fluffy and even. She had long since stopped trying not to step on the straw in her dirty boots. Beyond being impossible, it also didn't make much sense, since as soon as she cleaned out the first stall, its resident, the ancient mare she, uh, fed that morning, came in with muddy hooves. "All of my hard work," she said to her, patting her nose. The horse snuffed on her coat in response.

Now she was glad Keith had found her one of those plaid quilty jackets. It looked machine washable. Her jeans had gotten very dirty, especially after she knelt on the floor trying to clean up the contents of the wheelbarrow that had tipped over when she tried to move it. Still, the stalls were mucked and the manure was piled. She felt very farmy and very tired. She imagined this was what Cal and Luke and Libby and Katie went to bed feeling like every night, tired and satisfied with a job well done. And smelling like poop.

"You had her muck out *all* of the stalls on her own?"

To her credit, Miss Libby did not precisely hit him with the dish towel, although she looked like she would have hit him with a pot, given half the chance. She just sort of flapped it generally in his direction, albeit with menace and disapproval.

"She wanted something to do," Keith said lamely. He was just trying to be brotherly to his future sister-in-law. Of course, brotherly was not a feeling he had toward her when she bent over to pull on Luke's old boots. But she'd looked about ready to burst when he'd run into her outside the barn. He knew that feeling—that feeling you get when you want to run around and scream and pull up trees, but people expect you to just sit there nicely and *relax*. Keith was not good at *relaxing*. He liked to work.

Mal said she needed to work. So what if she ran to Miss Libby when she was done, complaining about him being a slave driver; so what if he was wrong about her. At least the stalls were clean. She did a pretty good job, too. He was kind of looking forward to turning over that chore.

"Keith Carson, I swear. When we have a guest in this house, you do not put them to *work*, no matter what they say. She came into the house smelling like—" Libby paused, waving the towel.

"Like horse shit?"

"I was trying to find a more ladylike word."

"Good thing I don't have to worry about that."

"You should still watch your mouth. We don't want Mal thinking we're a bunch of backward rednecks who can't speak properly."

Keith reflected briefly on Mal's generous use of language, especially when she tried to maneuver the too-full wheelbarrow for the first time. He was just coming into the barn to get a brush when he heard a string of the foulest curses he'd ever heard in his life—and he had grown up with cowboys.

He had poked his head around the doorway to see Mal struggling to right the wheelbarrow, then kneeling down in front of the spilled and very dirty straw. She sat there for a minute and Keith saw the tense set of her shoulders and thought maybe she was going to cry. He was about to go over and tell her she could go back into the house and clean up—anything to get her not to cry.

Then her shoulders rose and fell on a sigh and she leaned forward, scooping up armfuls of dirty straw and throwing it into the wheelbarrow. She was muttering to herself while she worked, and Keith couldn't hear it all, but he could definitely make out "Why don't you go shopping? We don't have any pigs here. I'm grumpy because my farm is going out of business and I don't have enough people to boss around and I'm an adult but I still live with my dad and I inhaled too much horse shit as a child so I'm incapable of decent human conversation." She started to kick the wheelbarrow, but apparently thought better of it because she paused midkick, then turned and kicked a stall door, letting out another string of curses.

No, they definitely didn't need to worry about Mal's virgin ears.

"Like I said, Lib, she wanted to help, so I let her."

"But *mucking out the stalls*. Didn't you have a more dignified chore for her?"

"There are no dignified chores. That's why they're called chores. Besides, don't you think she should get used to farm life if she's going to be marrying into this family?" That last part felt a little bitter on his tongue. Keith tried not to think about it.

Libby sighed. "I hope that Luke decides to settle down here with her. We still have those little cottages just sitting there like overgrown bushes. And you did such a nice job fixing up that little bunkhouse— who wouldn't want to live in a cute little place like that?"

"Lib, I don't think you should get your hopes up about Luke sticking around. He didn't even last twenty-four hours this time."

"Well, Mal certainly won't make a case for it if you keep asking her to do the dirty work. What's next? You gonna have her fixing fences?"

"No, Dad and Chase are doing that."

"Chase is here? Where is that boy? He didn't come in to get anything to eat before he went out."

"He didn't look like he was in a mood to talk to anyone."

"So naturally he jumped at the chance to go out with your father. Reach up and grab me that pot."

Keith did as he was told, then leaned back against the sink.

"You sure take after your daddy, strong and silent." Libby shook the colander full of potatoes. "But that doesn't mean you're off the hook, young man. Mal is a guest here, not free labor."

"I'm sorry if I made her mad; I really thought——"

Libby sighed as she dumped the potatoes into the pot on the stove. "No, she wasn't mad. She came in smelling to high heaven and smiling like a loon."

"So if she's not mad, why are you mad?"

"It's just not right, Keith, that's why."

"Miss Libby, it's all right." Mal stood in the kitchen doorway, wearing that floral skirt and socks, holding her dirty jeans. "I threatened him with bodily harm if he didn't give me something to do."

Her hair was still tied back in that messy ponytail, and she wore one of Luke's old sweatshirts with the sleeves rolled up at her wrists. She looked dead tired, and Keith had the sudden urge to go over to her, kiss those dark smudges from under her eyes.

Libby patting his arm broke his reverie. "All right, I'll forgive him. He always was a good boy." She crossed the kitchen, grabbing Mal's jeans, as she said, "to throw them in the wash presently."

To say an awkward silence descended on the kitchen would be an understatement. But Mal forged on, determined to——she wasn't sure what, exactly, but it seemed very important that Keith like her. Even though she wasn't entirely sure that she liked him. "So," she said, rocking back on her heels with forced casualness, "did the mucking pass muster?" She winced.

Keith rubbed the back of his neck, rocking back on his heels to mirror Mal. "Yeah, for a first-timer."

"Was there something wrong with my mucking? Should I go out and—"

Keith grabbed her arm as she headed out the door. To the barn. To re-muck. In her socks.

"It was great. Mal."

It felt sort of weird and intimate to hear her name coming from his mouth. He said it like it was a secret, just for the two of them. She turned, his hand still on her arm, but gentle.

"You did a great job," he repeated.

Then she was flush against him, her hips against his. Her nose against his teeth.

They looked at each other, stunned, for about half a second. Then Keith pulled her behind him and shouted, "No, Peanut! Out!" By the time Mal registered that she was still wearing the stupid stunned expression, that she was now pressed against Keith's back, and that the dog of which she was terrified was trying to lick her toes, Peanut was out the door, corralled by a stranger in a used-to-be white cowboy hat.

Inappropriate sexual tension was a great cure for fear of dogs.

Keith turned and cupped Mal's face in his hands.

"Mal? Mal, can you hear me? Are you going to throw up?"

She fluttered her hands in front of her face, brushing him away. "I'm OK," she said, keeping her eye nervously on the door.

"It's OK, Chase took Peanut out."

"Who?"

"Peanut. The dog. Do you remember?" He looked at her with concern, as if he thought she'd hit her head or something.

"I know Peanut. I mean, I am aware of Peanut."

"He makes sure of that."

"Who is Chase?"

"Oh. He works here."

No other information seemed to be forthcoming.

"He took Peanut out?"

"Yeah."

"Is Libby mad?"

"She doesn't know yet."

"Well, I'll say one thing for you. You have a loyal and affectionate dog."

"He's just excited because he hasn't seen me all day. Usually he's running around with me—"

Mal looked up at Keith, who suddenly had a guilty look on his face. *Oh,* she thought. *Oh.* "Did you keep Peanut out of the stables today because you knew I would be working there?"

Keith blushed. He blushed! It started in his neck and worked its way up and around to his ears. Very cute.

He looked at her, his eyes warm and green and questioning, and for a second she thought he was going to lean down and kiss her. She sort of hoped he would.

Abruptly, he stood up straight, turned on his heel, and went out the door.

Chapter 7

There were a lot of things Mal knew she shouldn't be doing. She shouldn't be lying to a perfectly nice family in Kentucky while her practically ex-husband pined away for her in his own maniacal way. She shouldn't be letting Miss Libby do her laundry or cook her meals without pitching in, although she was not entirely sure that one could be prevented.

The main thing she definitely should not be doing, though, was lusting after her fake fiancé's surly older brother.

He was rude and practically mute and really seemed to think she was an idiot.

But then he kept the dog out of sight because he knew she was afraid.

And he had really big hands.

Dammit.

Well, she thought as she shoved her feet into her shoes and followed Keith out the door, *the least I can do is make myself the smallest burden possible.*

She walked down the two steps from the kitchen door out into the yard. Libby's vegetable garden was to her right; maybe she could help weed later. *First things first, though,* she thought, walking toward the stables.

Keith was nowhere to be seen. But she did see the guy in the dirty hat who'd taken Peanut out. Peanut was also nowhere to be seen.

"Chase?" she asked, shielding her eyes from the afternoon sun.

He looked up at her curiously, then his face broke out into a million-dollar grin. He was tall and lanky, maybe even taller than Keith, with high cheekbones, a sharp jaw, and bright blue eyes that lit up when he smiled.

Was every man in Kentucky handsome? Did other women know about this?

"You must be Mal, Luke's girl."

She stopped in her tracks. "Well, I don't know if I'm his girl, per se."

"Sorry, Luke's woman?" He had a slightly bemused smile on his well-defined face. He was laughing at her. Or with her? She wasn't really laughing, but somehow, this guy made her feel like she was in on the joke.

"I like to think I'm my own woman."

"Oh, that's right, you're a Yankee. Sorry, let me put on my Yankee manners." He shook her hand firmly. "It's nice to meet you, as equals."

"You don't think Kentucky women are equals?"

"Sure I do, but I'm not going to tell them that."

She wasn't sure if that was sexist or charming. A little of both, probably. "Listen, I was wondering if you could help me with something."

"Sure, little lady." Now he was definitely teasing her.

"Knock it off, cowboy."

"Yes, ma'am."

She smiled. Ma'am. Nothing can make you feel old or disheveled like someone your own age calling you "ma'am."

"Chase, are you familiar with Peanut? The dog?"

"If you're talking about the three-legged mutt who tried to help me dig fence posts all morning while I tried to keep him from tripping up my horse, then, yes, I am familiar with Peanut."

"See, that's what I'm talking about. You don't usually take Peanut to, uh, work with you, do you?"

"No, ma'am," he said, starting to sound a little skeptical.

"Did Keith ask you to do that today?"

He was definitely skeptical now, if his charming face was any indication. "Yes."

"Do you know why?"

She swore she could see the gears turning in his head as he pondered whether or not he should admit that he knew about her fear of dogs, and potentially sell out his employer, or play dumb.

He didn't look like he was very good at playing dumb. Apparently he wasn't.

"Yes, ma'am," he said slowly, narrowing his eyes at her a little.

"That's why I need your help. I mean, if you have time. I can't let Keith disrupt his, I don't know, workflow, because I'm afraid of his dog. I mean, I appreciate it a lot. But he has to stop."

"So . . . do you want me to talk to him?"

"I think we both know that won't do any good." Chase nodded. "The only way he's going to stop accommodating my fear of dogs is if I'm not afraid of dogs anymore."

Chase blinked at her. She was smiling brightly, as if she was just suggesting something obvious, like the best way to get rid of your thirst was to have a drink. She could tell he didn't like where she was going. She had to talk fast.

"So I was thinking, since you're a farm guy and stuff, and you're pretty good with animals. Do you think you could, like, introduce me to Peanut? Just a little. I think if I get comfortable with him, it will be OK. Or at least Keith won't have to worry about me."

"I don't really think it's my place to—"

"Chase, I'm begging you. Everyone around here is treating me with kid gloves, like I'm, I don't know, a delicate flower or something. I'm not." She sighed. "But I am afraid of dogs. So if I could just get comfortable with this one dog—"

"Well, I don't really have time, Mal. I have a lot of other things to get done today."

Her face fell. "Oh, of course. I didn't think about that. Sorry, that was selfish. You're right, I'll just, ah, OK. Sorry."

Chase watched her walk back to the house. No wonder Luke was marrying her; if this was what saying no to her was like, he didn't think any man would ever be able to deny her anything.

He headed back into the barn to tell Keith that Luke's fiancée was starting to get ideas.

Mal did not go back into the kitchen. There was nothing for her in the kitchen, not since she could see Miss Libby working at the sink. Mal wouldn't even be allowed to dry a dish. There was definitely nothing for her in the stables, not unless she wanted to be scowled at. She wished she knew how to ride. This would be the perfect time to saddle up and ride 'em out. Or was that only for after you've robbed a bank?

She sighed and started to walk, not entirely sure where her legs would take her, but needing, well, distraction. Keith was just as high-handed and manipulative as Michael was. Maybe not as smooth about it, or maybe he was smoother. If she'd never discovered that he'd put Peanut out, then he would have that to hold over her. When really, it wasn't a good deed. She was afraid of dogs, so he should keep dogs away. Common decency. You don't have to be grateful for common decency.

That was a favorite saying of Michael's. He had used that one ever since she'd met him. The first time was in the dorm, in college. They had ordered pizza for an American History study session (it wasn't really a *study* session, what with the late night and the proximity to her tiny twin bed). When they were done eating, she cleared up the paper plates, taking the pizza box out to the big trash can in the hall. When she came back, Michael was leaning against her bed, taking notes from her notebook. She was a much better note-taker than he was. Especially since he went to only about a third of the lectures.

"You're welcome," she said sarcastically, picking up a stray napkin.

He put down the notebook, reached for her hand to pull her down. She kneeled next to him, their faces level.

"Babe, I paid for the pizza," he said, cupping her face. She had to look at him or it would seem like she was pouting. "It's only common decency that you should clean up. You're not owed any thanks when you do something that is just common decency."

That was not the most ridiculous thing she'd ever heard in her life, surely. But there was something about it that was so absurd, negotiating gratitude, keeping a tally of whose turn it was to do a good deed. She laughed—just a little one, but stopped when she saw Michael was serious.

"Fine, if you're going to be moody about it, I'll just go." He gathered his notebooks, shaking off her protests and her restraining hand. "You're welcome for the pizza," he shot back at her as he slammed the door.

Mal sat in the midst of papers and textbooks, staring dumbly at the door. They were just supposed to eat pizza, study, then make out. How had she screwed this up so badly? How had it ended with her studying the Civil War alone?

It didn't, really; Michael had taken her notebook.

Mal shook herself out of her reverie. She had put up with an absurd amount of emotional manipulation from Michael, and she wasn't going to do it again. Still, she couldn't keep herself from thinking about Michael and what he must be doing back in Maryland. He was in that big new house all alone—she wondered if he'd kept the decorator she had hired, if he was going to stick with the "touch of fabulous" she had been talked into for the master bathroom. She hoped, although she knew it was foolish, that he had forgotten about her, or at least moved on. Bunny Ashton-Pierce seemed poised to help him move on.

She tried not to spend too much time thinking about the improbably named Bunny, she of the fake boobs (Mal's were bigger, if not perkier) and the bottle blond hair done right (Mal was no competition there). Bunny of the spray tans and the charity auctions. The last time she had seen Bunny Ashton-Pierce was at a Botox party where she only shut up about how the laugh lines were her husband's fault—he was always such a cutup—to get an injection in the corner of her mouth. Mal didn't quite remember Dr. Ashton-Pierce being a cutup. More of a handsy perv with an apparent fondness for natural breasts, but she'd sat silently in the corner, hoping no one would notice her since she was not too fond of needles and, frankly, had earned every damn laugh line on her face. Not that there were many. More of a fine suggestion of a laugh line to come.

She didn't have as many wrinkles around her eyes as, say, Keith did. But it was different for a man. Keith looked rugged with wrinkles, just like he would probably look distinguished with gray hair. Jerk.

Anyway, Keith was a bully, just like Michael. Oh, maybe he wasn't as outright manipulative as Michael was, and he didn't seem to have Michael's temper, but the way he patronized her, tested her with crappy (literally!) chores, kept Peanut away without telling her. The last thing she needed to do was put up with another bully.

Mal stopped just short of the fence she was about to run into. She was pissed off, mostly at Keith for treating her like she was an idiot. No, mostly at herself for allowing herself to be treated like an idiot. Anyway, maybe she was overreacting to Keith——the last time he'd seen her with the dog, she had practically thrown up in his lap.

No. She shook her head, determined. The minute she started rationalizing his behavior, that was the minute she lost control of her life again. She wasn't going to let another man have that power over her, not since she had finally taken these few tentative steps away from Michael. Besides, what was Keith to her? Nothing. He was her fake future brother-in-law, just some dumb hick farmer with big hands and a nice butt.

Dammit.

She stopped suddenly at the sound of Peanut's high-pitched bark. Mal had practically walked right into him, but he was on the other side of the fence.

She froze.

Then she looked at Peanut, his wet nose poking between the wide boards. He got down low, digging with his one front paw, leaning over to his side, trying to burrow beneath the fence. His tail was wagging manically. It looked like his butt was going to take off.

It was sort of funny. Sort of cute. Peanut wasn't scary. Just, well, energetic.

"You're nothing but a big bully, too, you know." Mal thought about how long she'd been afraid, how she'd cross the street when she saw her neighbors out walking their dogs. Little dogs, who couldn't attack her restrained on a leash and, even if they could, could do nothing more than bite her ankles. She rubbed the scar on her chin. She had been a kid. That dog was old, sitting in the sun, and she was just petting him. No, she was trying to get him to play, but he was old and wanted to sleep. Now she could see it clearly, the dog trying to inch away, but she kept tossing him the ball, pulling his collar when he wouldn't chase it. So he nipped her chin and scared the hell out of her. He hadn't really hurt her; she needed three stitches and had a scar smaller than some people's acne scars. She hadn't known anything about dogs, still didn't. Except now she knew to leave them alone when they wanted to be left alone.

Peanut, clearly, did not want to be left alone.

During her reverie, Peanut had calmed down. He sat looking at her, panting, his front paw on the fence rail. It sort of looked like he was smiling.

"You're pretty cute for a bully, aren't you?"

He tilted his head, giving her that curious dog look.

Mal took a deep breath. Even if she didn't become best friends with Peanut, she couldn't have every member of the Carson family, and apparently everyone who worked on the farm, spending their energy keeping her and the dog apart.

"How about a truce? You don't eat me, and I won't throw up every time I see you."

Peanut let out a little bark.

"OK." She took another deep breath, steeling herself. She took a step forward, letting Peanut smell her hand. She must have smelled good, because he licked her. She flinched back and Peanut jumped off the fence and took a step backward.

"Oh, OK. You didn't mean to scare me. You're just being a dog. Dogs lick." She wiped her hand on her jeans. "No offense." She smiled ruefully. Peanut took a step toward the fence.

Mal squatted down, stuck her hand between the rails. "Can I pet you?" Peanut shoved his head into her outstretched hand. "I'll take that as a yes," she said, and began to stroke his head. When she scratched behind his ears, Peanut flopped to the ground, his three legs in the air. "Well, there's no need to be such a slut about it." But she laughed, and reached through to scratch his belly.

"If I come through this fence, are you going to jump on me? Or can we take this slow?" Peanut tilted his curious head again, then let his tongue loll out to the side. "I guess you probably don't speak English. OK, here I come." She moved to the gate, just a few yards away. When she opened it, Peanut was there. He didn't jump on her; maybe he did speak English. He just shoved his big body against her legs, then dropped to the ground again, rolling his stomach up to her. Mal laughed, then squatted down next to him and rubbed his belly.

While she was making friends, one of the horses had come up to them. Peanut rolled up and sniffed the horse's snout. The horse put his nose in Mal's hair and snorted. She put her hand to the side of his face.

"I feel like Snow White," she said, half expecting a bunny, and then maybe a bird to sit on her shoulder. Peanut licked her cheek. "But maybe with a few more germs."

The horse lost interest in her pretty fast, and she let it go. She was too happy with Peanut, who rolled onto the ground and let her scratch and scratch and scratch. Then he got up, picked up a stick, and nudged her hand.

"OK! OK, I get it. Here you go."

She was about to throw the stick when she saw Katie come charging out of the barn.

"Who left the damn gate open?" she shouted, sprinting past Mal and Peanut, who gave friendly chase. Mal turned to watch Katie go, an apology on her lips, when she saw the friendly horse. On the other side of the fence. Running toward the road.

Chapter 8

Mal wasn't sure she had ever seen any person run as fast as Katie did, heading toward the main gate and the dirt road. She stood there dumbly, not quite taking in what was going on. Katie kept yelling, "Horse loose," and, sure, there was a part in the back of Mal's mind that understood that she had left the gate open and that, because of her, a horse was running toward the road and freedom, but that part of her mind was not connected to the part that told her legs to go, to run after Katie and, when she eventually caught up (dang, that girl was fast!), help.

There was also the part of her mind that was distracted by the sight she caught out of the corner of her eye, of Keith racing out of the barn, swinging up on a saddle, and charging past her. He didn't pause exactly, but he turned and shouted at her to "Come on!" So she ran after him.

Miss Libby was standing closest to the front gate, waving a big white sheet. Chase had run up and closed the front gate, and Keith was dismounting, standing a few yards away. The horse charged up, and Mal thought for sure Libby was going to be trampled. But she waved and shouted and the horse turned, first to the right, where Keith was waving his arms, then to the left, where Katie was doing the same thing. Then toward Mal.

"Wave your arms and make a lot of noise!" Keith shouted at her. So she did. She felt like an idiot, but it seemed to be doing the trick, because the waving Carsons were coming up behind the horse, closing the circle and slowly moving toward the barn.

When the horse was back in her stall (Bob was her name. A girl horse named Bob.), Keith went in there with her, toweling off her shivering muscles with a blanket, speaking soothing words. Chase was putting Keith's horse back in his stall, putting up the saddle. Libby went back to the house to finish hanging the laundry out (which explained the sheet) and told them supper was in ten minutes. Katie just stood at the stall gate, fuming.

"Who the hell left the gate open?" she demanded.

"Cool off, Katie," Chase said softly.

Katie stomped her foot, and Bob mimicked her. "It was Mal, wasn't it? What the hell was she doing with the horses anyway? I know she's from the suburbs, but how stupid do you have to be to miss the basic common sense to close the gate behind you so the damn horses don't run into the road!"

"Katie!" Keith had raised his voice to a grown-up authority voice. It wasn't much louder, but it still silenced Katie. "Knock it off. This isn't the first time Bob got out, and it won't be the last. So let it go, leave Mal out of this, and go help Libby with dinner."

"Oh, I see, you just want to send the woman back to the kitchen!"

"No, I want to get you out of this damn barn so you stop spooking Bob."

Katie paused at that. She gave Bob a scratch on the nose. She was still a little agitated, but she stomped appreciatively. So did Bob. Katie turned to Keith. "Fine. I'll go help Libby but only because I'm starving and I want to eat. From now on, you're in charge of babysitting Luke's little stray."

"Watch it, Katie."

Katie turned and jumped gracefully over a pile of tack before continuing her storming, petulant exit toward the house.

Mal was not so graceful. Trying to sneak out of the barn, she tripped over the tack in the stall she had been hiding in. She landed, gracefully, she hoped, on her face. Scrambling up, she looked over to see Keith and Bob, their heads poking out of the stall.

"I was just, uh, I was just going. I'm going to go," she said, and ran toward the house.

Dinner that evening was a tense affair. Mal knew it was her fault, but nobody would even look at her. Libby had told Mal that usually when one of the Carson children did something wrong, they would be crushed under the weight of their father's disapproving gaze, then punished, then comforted by Miss Libby. But Mal was not one of the Carson children and leaving the gate open was not her fault, really. She didn't know.

In between saying grace and passing the chicken wings, Cal said, "Nobody let that girl go about on her own until she learns how it's done."

It was not said unkindly, not entirely, but Mal thought she probably would have preferred if he went back to ignoring her. She bristled. Another bully.

"Yeah, next time I might burn down the barn or muck out the feed pile." And then she laughed, a short, tense sound. Looking at the blank faces around the table, she thought maybe it was too soon for jokes. So she kept her head down, dug into her food, and waited for the meal to be over.

As soon as she could politely excuse herself from the table, which was about half an hour after she wanted to, she went up to her room—Luke's room—and dug around in her bag for her cell phone. She had bought it at a big box store around Morgantown. It was one of those really basic pay-as-you-go phones. She had put a hundred dollars worth of minutes on it, figuring it would be good for emergencies, but also feeling a little like a drug dealer since she could throw the phone out any time she wanted. Untraceable.

She had yet to use it, although she had given Luke the number. He hadn't used it either, hadn't called since he'd been gone, but she needed him now. She needed to talk to him, and she needed him to get her out of here.

The sun had set while they were eating dinner, and as Mal stepped out on the front porch, her breath stopped at the blue glow of twilight, the first stars dotting the sky. She hadn't been this far from the city in a long time, and she didn't realize how much she had been missing the stars. She took a deep breath of the crisp evening air, wrapped her scarf more firmly around her neck, and called Luke.

It rang and rang, and while it rang, she saw Libby pull back the curtain and, seeing it was Mal on the porch, give a friendly wave. Mal smiled and waved back, then stepped off the porch. She didn't need anyone in the family to hear this conversation. She started walking.

If there is a conversation, she thought, hoping not to have to deal with voice mail. She hated voice mail.

Luke finally picked up, sounding a little breathless. "Mal? What's wrong?" There was a lot of noise behind him, as if he was in a crowd. Maybe a bar.

"Nothing! I'm fine. I just wanted to talk to you, that's all."

"Mal."

She heard one distinctive voice above the rest. "Luke, are you at an auction or something?"

"What? No! No, I'm at a party."

"It sounds like an auctioneer in the background."

"That's just, a party trick. Hold on, let me go outside." She heard a few mumbled "excuse me's" and "hey, back in a minute," and then the noise of the crowd faded. She could hear him perfectly. "What's going on, baby?"

"It's nothing, really, I just wanted to say hi. Hi."

"Hi. Mal."

There was no use. She burst out crying. "Your family hates me. I let a horse out. I threw up at the dog." As if speaking of the devil, Peanut came off the kitchen steps and nuzzled his nose into her free hand. The dog, at least, forgave her. She kept walking, Peanut trotting beside her. "The only thing I'm doing right here is eating Miss Libby's cooking and mucking out stables."

"Why are you mucking out the stables? That's a disgusting job."

"Please, Luke, it's the only thing I've done right so far, unless Keith is too polite to tell me I've done it wrong. He's probably in the barn right now, re-mucking everything. Jerk."

Luke laughed softly. "Baby, trust me. Keith is not too polite to tell you when you've done something wrong."

She warmed at that. Maybe she wasn't entirely useless. Then she remembered how Keith had kept Peanut away without telling her, so maybe he *was* too polite. Then she remembered how he'd swung up on that horse to go chasing after Bob. She shook her head. That was not a very polite thought.

She focused back on the phone. She was supposed to be talking to her fiancé. Fake fiancé, but still.

"Tell me about the rest. How did you let a horse out? Did they get it back?"

"Yeah, it was Bob. I left the gate open."

"Why would you leave the gate open at a farm?"

"I didn't think! This is exactly how your family is treating me, like this should be common sense. But it's not common sense if you've never been on a farm before!"

The more she thought about it, though, the more she came to realize it really was common sense. Horses were fenced in for a reason. She felt like an idiot.

"OK, OK, you're right. They should have explicitly told you not to leave the gates open."

"Stop, don't patronize me. I know I did something really stupid. I'm just having trouble coming to terms with it. Give me a minute."

"It was Bob that got out?"

"Yeah."

"Well, I wouldn't worry about it. When Bob was young and could actually run fast, she got out at least once a week. That horse has serious wanderlust."

"Bob the Girl Horse."

"Yeah, she's Katie's. When Dad brought her home as a filly, her name was Princess. Katie flipped—you should have seen her. It was amazing. She kicked this tin bucket clear across the yard and shouted, 'I'm not riding a horse named Princess!' Cal was pissed."

"She seems attached to the horse now."

"Oh, she loves that horse. The next morning, we found Katie asleep in the stall. She announced that she loved the horse and that she was going to name her Bob. No matter how hard we tried to convince her that Bob was not a girl's name, she stuck to it." He laughed again. "She really loves that horse."

"That explains why she bit my head off when she saw her get out." That wasn't entirely true. Katie had bitten Mal's head off behind her back, so to speak. To her face, she was very polite, and very cold.

"She'll get over it. Katie gets a little bit hot, but she'll calm down. If she doesn't apologize to you, I'll talk to her."

"No! No, that's fine." Katie did not seem like the kind of woman who appreciated being forced into anything. "You don't have to talk to Katie about me. In fact, you don't have to talk to anyone about me." She took a deep breath. "Luke, this was a ridiculous idea."

"Come on, Mal."

"No, listen! It makes no sense that you would just show up with a fiancée."

"I've never told my family everything I've done. This is nothing."

"Thanks."

"You know what I mean."

"Well, even if that's true, I think the plausibility of the story has been compromised since, what did Cal say to Libby, you up and left me! How do you expect anyone to believe that we're madly in love if you don't stick around to act madly in love with me?"

"You're not mooning over me in my absence?"

"Luke, I'm serious."

"I know, I know. Yes, this is a serious flaw in the plan here. But I had an opportunity I couldn't pass up. I'll be back in a week or so, and then we'll figure out what to do."

"A week?"

Luke cleared his throat. "A week or so, yeah."

"Luke, I can't stay here alone for another week! Katie will freeze me to death!"

"I told you that would blow over."

"That's easy for you to say, you grew up with her. And you're on the other end of a phone line, so you didn't have to eat dinner with her."

"I do miss Libby's suppers."

"She'd be happy to cook you whatever you want. Please, Luke." She heard him sigh. He was clearly not going to give in. "Please. I'm going out of my mind here. I'm walking on eggshells. Everything I do is wrong. I might as well go back to Michael."

"Don't even joke about that, Mal. My family may be a little prickly." Mal snorted in response to that. "But, baby, Michael is an asshole."

Mal didn't say anything.

"Do you remember the state you were in when I met you? You were walking into things from looking over your shoulder. You couldn't take a dump without asking permission first."

"Luke. It wasn't like that."

"So he didn't call you a bunch of horrible names and expect you to make him dinner while he went upstairs and screwed his new girl-friend? And don't you dare tell me that he only hit you once. Once was enough."

She closed her eyes. Once was more than enough. The idea of returning to DC turned her stomach—her body remembered even if her mind was a little slow on the uptake. "No, he did those things."

"Listen, my family, they're tough. They work hard, and they don't meet a lot of people who are not like them. You have to give them time to get used to you."

"How much time?"

"And you have to stand up for yourself. Katie especially will bully you into the ground before she even knows what she's doing. Keith and Cal will probably ignore you for a while, but you have to stand up to Katie."

Keith wasn't ignoring her, she thought. She stood up to him. But the pity party felt too good to be over.

"Even Libby was giving me disappointed looks all through dinner."

"You probably weren't eating enough. Baby, it will be fine. You just have to give it time. I'll be back soon—"

"A week or so is not soon."

"It's soon enough. Then we'll sort it out. We'll go somewhere great, a tropical island."

She laughed into the phone. "How are we going to get to a tropical island? I barely had enough money to get us here."

"You think I can't take care of my woman?" He really played up the twang, so "can't" came out like "cain't."

She laughed again. "Luke, you realize we aren't really engaged, right?"

"I'm still gonna take care of you. Now, what's this about you throwing up on that mutt?"

She looked down at Peanut, who had been silently trotting beside her, and patted his head. He rolled in the dirt. "We're working on our relationship." She laughed, and told him the story. Told him how she was afraid for no real reason, how Keith was so nice to her and it pissed her off, how she took charge and how Peanut was, at the moment, her favorite Carson.

By the time she was done, she felt better. Sure, she had alienated all of the human inhabitants of the farm, but the dog liked her. Her phone beeped in her ear. "Luke, I think my battery is dying. Stupid cheap phone."

"Plug it in, I'll wait."

She stopped, looked around. "Uh, I'm not at the house. I was sort of wandering." She was standing a few yards from the cutest little house, a bungalow with big green shutters and a very inviting front porch. "I'm at a little cottage or something."

"Baby, you really wandered. Go back to the house before it gets too dark to see. They don't have street lights, you know."

"Ha, ha. Fine, I'm going. Hey, thanks."

"Good night, baby."

Mal swore she could hear that smile in his voice. She hung up and looked down at Peanut. "Are you ready to play Lassie? Which way is home, boy?"

He barked up at her, then turned quickly to the cottage, barking again.

"What is it, boy? Is there someone in the well?" That was a good one; if only the dog wasn't the only one to hear it.

There wasn't someone in the proverbial well, but there was someone in the cottage.

Keith was rooting around in the overgrown garden for the false rock that held the key before he was even fully aware that he was at the cottage. Something about that tense dinner had sent him outside after helping Libby clean up. The way Katie stared daggers at Mal, who looked like she wanted to crawl under the table with Peanut, the way no one—not Cal, not Libby, and certainly not him—came to Mal's defense. He was ashamed but also annoyed. Who leaves a gate open when there are horses that can get out?

Someone who, as Mal admitted, has never been on a farm before.

He grunted in victory as he found the key—at least something was going right for him tonight. He walked into the kitchen, which was not in as bad shape as he'd feared it would be. The fridge was empty—small favors—but the electricity was still on. He turned on the lights, seeing a thin layer of dust over the stovetop. He stopped, picturing Vanessa standing over the stove, canning peaches from the tree out back. She loved making things from scratch, called herself a domestic diva. The curtains, now faded and dirty, were the first thing she'd made when they moved in. He remembered that day so clearly—him coming in from the barn. The Smith kids had just come to pick up their ancient cat, Muffin, who was fully recovered from whatever the hell was wrong with her. He'd knocked his boots on the mat and Vanessa had scolded him to stop. Going across the kitchen anyway, standing behind her, putting his hands protectively over her stomach.

"You going to the doctor today?"

She looked up at the clock. "In about an hour. I've got time to finish this batch, make myself presentable, and then I'll head into town."

He bent down to kiss her neck. "Is that all you've got time for?"

"Keith Carson, leave me be! I've got work to do!" She laughed and turned to kiss him, then shooed him out of the kitchen.

Was that really how it happened? His memories seemed infused with a haze of light, like they were a movie shot with one of those soft filters they used on aging divas. None of it seemed real. Did they ever fight? Vanessa was always so willing to get her hands dirty, always having dinner ready for him, doing projects around the house. He'd come home one day to find her pulling apart the guest bedroom.

"What are you doing?" he'd asked, lifting the dresser that she had caught on the rug. Her hair was pulled back in a bandana, her jeans dusty.

"Making room," she said, out of breath. "Do you think your dad still has that rocker up in the attic?"

"What are you talking about, the rocker? Hold on, give me that," he said, taking the mirror from her.

She finally stopped, looked up at him. "This is going to be the nursery."

"I know, we talked about that, but I thought we decided we wouldn't worry about changing it over until——"

Keith stopped, realization dawning on him. "Do we need to build a nursery, baby?"

He vaguely recalled whooping, swinging her up in his arms, kissing her breathless.

The nursery was never finished. On the way back from her appointment, she ran into Butch Wallis. More accurately, Butch Wallis ran into her. He had had a rough day, wife was nagging him, tried to find comfort in a bottle. He was dried out now, found Jesus in prison. He wrote Keith a letter every year asking for forgiveness, and Keith threw every one of them away. Butch Wallis had lost control of his damn car, run into his wife. She died instantly, the state trooper said, which was supposed to make him feel better. She died instantly, and so did their child. He never knew if it was a boy or a girl.

The fog around him burst, the light filter he saw his memories through vanished, and he was left with the harsh glare of reality in the form of a naked bulb hanging from the ceiling of his child's half-finished nursery. The rocker sat in the corner. The rocker that his mother had rocked him on, that Vanessa was supposed to rock their baby on. He sat on the rocker, picked up a half-finished knit blanket out of a basket, buried his face in it. He rocked back and forth, clenching his eyes against tears for his lost wife, his lost child, his lost life. Weeping for the half-life he had been living for the past three years. Weeping for Peanut's lost leg, for Luke's lack of direction, for his father's poor health. Tears for being so shabby to his little brother's fiancée because he didn't know how else to act if he was going to be in the same room with her.

His head came up when he heard a soft gasp. There she was, standing in the doorway of the nursery, her blondish hair a mess, scarf wrapped tight around her neck, her hand over her mouth in surprise.

"I'm sorry! I didn't know anyone was in here. I saw the light on and I thought—"

"Get out of here," Keith growled. He didn't want anyone in here, least of all her, this woman who made him forget his vows to his wife, this woman who was going to make those same vows to his brother.

He thought he saw her lower lip tremble. She soldiered on. "Keith, I am so sorry. About the horse, about coming here—what is this place? Like I said, I saw the light and—"

"Mal. Get out."

She looked alarmed. Maybe he had shouted; he didn't know. He just had to get her out of this room.

"Sorry," she whispered, then turned and left.

Keith rocked back, leaning his head on the back of the rocker, collecting himself. After a minute, he got up, folded the blanket, and turned out all the lights on his way out. He put the key back and started home. He would have to apologize to Mal when he got there. He would like to never see her again—no, he would like to never have laid eyes on her. But he could man up, especially after a long walk in the chilly fall air.

"I don't know the way back."

He started, then his eyes adjusted and he saw Mal standing by the door in the dark.

"What?"

"I tried to do what you asked." He had growled it, really. "I tried to go home, but I don't know the way and I can't see the house from here. It wasn't dark when I walked over."

"Oh."

"I'm sorry, I know you want to be alone. That's why I went walking—to be alone. Well, Peanut came with me, but he's good company. Anyway, I don't trust him to get me home."

"Peanut knows the way," he said, too stunned to say anything more intelligent. "So, you're not afraid of dogs?"

"I am. I'm not afraid of Peanut, though. We came to an understanding."

Peanut nudged her leg, then ran off. Keith noticed he ran in the direction of the house. Some understanding.

"OK, let's go." He started walking, and she fell into step beside him.

They walked in silence for a while, her head held low, his hands shoved in his pockets.

Finally she looked up at him and asked him the question he knew was coming. "What is that place?" She shivered a little.

"Are you cold?"

"I'm always cold." She was wearing just a thin jacket, and her scarf seemed more fashion than function. The temperature had dropped since the sun had gone down; even he was a little cold in his quilted barn fleece.

But he had to stop being a jerk to her. Not just because she was going to be family, but because she hadn't done anything wrong, not really wrong, not enough to justify the way they were all freezing her out. She was a nice girl, probably, and she seemed committed to Luke. She deserved a chance.

He took off his coat, draped it over her shoulders. She protested, even as she snuggled into it, wrapping it tighter around her. He said he was fine, shoved his hands back into his pockets. They walked back to the house in silence.

Chapter 9

The next morning, Mal walked into the stables determined to be helpful. She'd mucked yesterday; she could muck today.

Keith and Katie were already in there, and already mucking.

"Hey, that's my job!" she called.

Katie turned. "Did you close the gate?"

"No, I thought someone else——"

"Dammit, Mal!" she shouted, and dropped her pitchfork to head for the door.

"Katie!" Keith shouted after her. Then, when she turned, "She's joking."

Mal smiled up at him.

"You are joking, right?"

"Yes, I closed the gate. I may not have common sense, but I'm a fast learner. Thanks for the vote of confidence, Katie."

"Katie, I have to do some paperwork. Can you and Mal finish up here?"

Katie looked at her brother like he'd suggested she give up one of her kidneys. Or wear a dress and heels. Keith didn't see, or preferred not to, and he left them to the chores.

Katie sighed and looked her over. "That was kind of mean, just there." She smiled and handed Mal the pitchfork. "Welcome to the family."

They laughed and they mucked.

"Listen, Katie. I'm sorry about yesterday. It was stupid to leave the gate open."

Katie wheeled a bag of feed outside, much more gracefully than Mal could have managed.

"Yeah. It was. But maybe I was a little hard on you."

"Maybe? Libby had to reheat my dinner, you were giving me such a cold shoulder."

"OK, I was a bitch. It's just that you're a lot to take in."

Mal raised her eyebrow.

"Luke has never been one to commit. He even had more than one prom date. So when he showed up, engaged, that was a shock."

"I wanted him to call ahead at least, give you some time to prepare."

"And you're not at all like who he usually dates."

"Who does he usually date?"

"Country girls. Stupid girls with big boobs. Blondes."

Mal smiled. "Well, I'm glad that you don't think I'm stupid. Although I'm shocked that my dye job hasn't fooled you."

"I don't advocate spending a lot of time on beauty care, but you really need to get that hair fixed."

"No salons in Hollow Bend."

"I know a guy. Jack—we went to high school together. That's his horse on the end." She indicated a mostly white horse with brown spots—appaloosa, Mal remembered. "He'll help you."

"Thanks. That's really nice. And thanks for letting me follow you around."

"Well, you were right, you are a quick learner. Anyway, after lunch we want to go to the Harvest Festival. Are you coming?"

"Oh, I don't know anything about it."

"Libby didn't tell you? Well, I'll let it be a surprise. I have to go early. Some of my kids are showing."

What? "What?"

"Oh, right, not a country girl. Some of the kids show pigs and sheep. I help with the horses. You didn't have 4-H in DC?"

"Not exactly."

"I'll bet. So I'm going to go over when we're done. Keith will take you later."

"Does Keith know about that plan?"

"Who cares? He'll do it."

"You seem to be very sure of that."

"If you don't make him take you, he's going to sit at that computer all day, cursing at invoices. So he's going to miss out on sunshine and fried cheesecake and then he's going to be a pain in the butt because even though he pretends he doesn't like to socialize, he does want to go to this."

Fried cheesecake? "I just don't know if he'll want to take me. We had sort of a weirdness last night."

"A weirdness? What kind of weirdness?"

"I went for a walk and I ran into him in this little house thing over there." She pointed in what she thought was the general direction of the little house thing. "He was not pleased that I was there. It was very gothic."

"You went in?"

"I heard a noise. I thought you were being burgled."

"You thought there was a criminal in the 'little house thing,' so you went inside."

"Yes. Yesterday was my day of stupid decisions. I'm much better today, I promise."

"Well, no one really goes in there but him. It's his house."

"I thought he lived in that bunkhouse."

"He does. He does now. He used to live in that house with his wife."

"He's married?"

Katie shook her head. "Didn't Luke tell you any of this?"

Now Mal shook her head.

"He's a widower," Katie said. "His wife died about three years ago. She was hit by a drunk driver."

"Oh! That's terrible."

"That's an understatement. We were all devastated. Vanessa, that's his wife, she was amazing. She was a real farm girl, and she was really fun. She made Keith fun. She was like a big sister to me."

"I'm sorry." *Vanessa fit right in*, Mal thought.

"Well, it was a long time ago."

"Not that long ago, Katie."

"Keith will never get over her. He was a vet, did you know that? He was working with Dr. Monroe in town, was going to take over his practice when he retired. He fixed Peanut."

"Fixed him?"

"Yeah, Keith found Peanut in a ditch. Literally in a ditch. He had been hit by a car, and probably abused a lot more before then. Such a tiny little runt. Keith couldn't save his leg, but he saved his life."

"No wonder Peanut is so loyal."

"It's that or the bacon. Peanut is sort of a slut for bacon."

Keith wandered up to the side of the barn, rubbing his eyes.

"Katie, Libby says if you want lunch before you go, it's ready."

"OK. See you later, Mal."

"See you."

Mal watched Katie run off, then turned to Keith. Keith the Jerk. Keith the Vet Who Saved Helpless Animals. Keith the Widower.

"What?" he asked.

"Nothing," she said. "Nothing."

Chapter 10

Keith didn't even bother trying to find a spot close to the fair's entrance—they were about six hours too late for that. The Harvest Festival attracted people from all over the county, and for the past few years, it had even started to catch on with hipster families in Lexington. It was barely recognizable as the glorified 4-H-show-with-funnel-cake Keith had grown up with. Cal muttered something along the same lines as Keith pulled his truck in line next to a tall yellow flag.

"Remember where we parked," Libby reminded them. She turned to Mal. "Last year we were walking around for about two hours trying to find Cal's truck. We eventually had to get a ride home and come back the next day when all the other cars were gone."

"Who are all these people anyway?" Cal grumbled. "This used to be a day for the *town*, not for rich people from Lexington. Come down here in their *SUVs*. 'Let's go look at the rednecks!'"

"Oh, Cal, you are *not* a redneck," Libby said, patting him gently on his red neck. "Let's go see if my pie won this year."

Mal's mouth watered just remembering. She'd woken up to the smell of apple pie baking. When she'd come, drooling, into the kitchen, Libby was pulling two pies out of the oven to sit on the windowsill—one for judging, one for the family.

As Mal helped her push the table and several chairs in front of the sill (Peanut was a pretty good jumper), Libby explained that because of the long summer, she had some raspberries left, and by some miracle (her words), the deer hadn't eaten all the pears off the tree in the side yard, so she'd experimented with an apple-pear-raspberry pie. It wasn't the sort of thing that usually won pie contests, but for the past couple of years, Libby said, the judges were looking for something more exciting than the same old flaky crust and traditional homemade insides.

"If those rich people from Lexington would stay out of this, a man would be able to get a decent piece of apple pie, none of this fancy-fruit concoction stuff."

Of course, Cal had eaten two pieces of the "fancy-fruit concoction" for breakfast.

Libby laughed as Cal got out of the truck and opened her door. Keith was just reaching for Mal's door when she shoved it open, hitting him in the nose.

"Oh! Sorry! I didn't see you!"

"I'm fine," he mumbled.

Mal was just looking toward the entrance to the fair, which seemed to be about sixteen miles away, when the tractor acting as a shuttle bus pulled up. It was pulling a wagon full of hay and passengers that rocked and creaked even when the tractor wasn't moving. Cal hoisted Libby up, who laughed and swatted his hands at her waist. Keith looked like he was about to toss Mal in behind them, so she blurted out, "I'll walk."

Keith paused, looked at the mostly full hay wagon, shrugged, and started to walk with her.

The shuttle was hardly an express, and as Keith and Mal strolled along, the tractor barely kept up with them. The driver—who was chewing straw, Mal was pleased to see—kept turning around to yell at the kids to keep their hands in the wagon. They looked like the fancy Lexington people Cal disliked so much—Mal recognized their expensive kiddie footwear as a popular brand in the DC suburbs.

They walked much as they had the night before, Keith with his hands shoved into his pockets, both of them silent. Mal tried not to let it get to her. She had never been to a real country fair before, just those suburban ones where they close off a couple of streets and put rides on the courthouse lawn. This was on, like, fairgrounds. In a cow field.

It was a good thing one of them was paying attention. Keith grabbed her arm and steered her around the worst of the danger.

"Keith? Keith Carson, how are you?"

Mal looked up to see a well-past-middle-aged man reach out of the wagon (to the consternation of the driver) and shake Keith's hand.

"Dr. Monroe. Not bad, you?"

"I'm fine, I'm fine. This Luke's girl?" he asked, indicating Mal.

"Yes, this is Mal. Mal, Dr. Monroe."

"Mal, nice to meet you. Luke's a lucky man."

"Me, too," said Mal. "Well, the lucky part."

"Mal, this is my daughter, Billie." He indicated a pretty redhead across the wagon. She waved.

"Hi! Hi, Keith. Katie here?"

"Yeah. 4-H." Billie nodded in what Mal assumed was understanding. They were speaking Hollow Bend shorthand.

"Mal, I need you to do me a favor," Dr. Monroe said, leaning out of the wagon a little. Mal stepped closer—she didn't think the wagon was up for much leaning. "Now that you're part of that family, I need to see if you can't talk this brother-in-law of yours into going back into business, letting an old man retire."

Mal looked at Keith, who reddened, but didn't slow his pace.

"I'm sure you know he was a fine veterinarian. You still got that mutt you fixed up?"

Poor Peanut, Mal thought. *Always "that mutt."*

"Keith used to do all the books, too. Billie gave it a try, but—"

"I prefer guts to numbers," Billie said.

"I used to be a bookkeeper," Mal said. *Shut up, Mal. What are you going to do, get a job? Put down fake roots with your fake fiancé?*

"Well!" Dr. Monroe looked enormously pleased. "If you and Luke decide to stick around, I might have to persuade Luke to let you come work for me."

"I think she can make her own mind up about that," Keith mumbled.

Mal thought, *I was just about to say that.*

"Now, Doc, you let that poor girl alone. We want her to stick around," shouted Libby from the back of the wagon.

The doctor laughed, then lurched forward as the tractor came to a stop to try to squeeze more passengers on. Mal waved, then she and Keith kept going.

"I used to be a vet," Keith said after a moment.

"Katie said."

"What else did she say?"

"Well, she explained what you were doing in the cottage when I found you the other night."

Keith kicked a rock out of the way, cursed under his breath.

"Listen, Keith. I know you don't like me butting into your business, and I'm trying really hard to stay out of it. In fact, I'd like to stay out of your entire family's business. But this is my first serious fair, and I want to soak it all in. So do you think we can call a truce or something? Or if you have to scowl at me, can you wait until my back is turned?"

Keith rubbed the back of his neck, then looked up at Mal. And he smiled. The wrinkles around his eyes got deeper, but his eyes blazed bright and green. He didn't look so tired anymore.

"Truce," he said, shaking her outstretched hand.

"Whoa," she said. "You're smiling. You should do it more often."

"Yes, ma'am," he said, then led her around another cow pie, and kept on walking toward the fair.

The hardest part of eating food on a stick, Mal decided later, was choosing where to begin. For an hors d'oeuvre, she considered an ear of corn, but ultimately went with the pickle on a stick. Next she was tempted by the hot bologna on a stick, but every time she said it, she blushed, so she went for the chicken leg wrapped in bacon.

She thought she was going to die, and she couldn't have been happier.

"This is the best meal on a stick I've ever had in my life," she said, leaning her back against the edge of the worn picnic table they were sharing with a very messy, very happy family of five. She stretched her legs out and gave a deep sigh.

Keith, who was washing down his lamb on a stick with a good old-fashioned corn dog, said, "I thought you'd never had food on a stick before."

"Shh," she said, tilting her head back and closing her eyes. "I'm too full for witty retorts."

The little boy sitting across the table from her had been playing peek-a-boo with his corn dog, but gave up when Keith started to play. Now, though, the little guy wanted to play again with Mal, whose back was to him. So he hit her on the head. With his corn dog.

"Oh! Oh, I'm so sorry! Brayden! Look what you've done!" gasped Brayden's mother.

"Don't worry about it," Mal said, reaching back to pat her hair, and coming back with a handful of mustard.

"Here, use some of these," Brayden's mother said, unwrapping a wet wipe and reaching for Mal's head.

"That's OK," Mal said, intercepting her hand. "I've got it. Seriously, it's no big deal. It's just mustard."

"It blends in with your dye job," Keith said. Then he clapped his hand over his mouth.

Mal looked at him, his eyes wide, looking like he wanted to pull those words back into his mouth. She knew that feeling very well. Besides, he looked so young like that, so different from his usual scowly self.

She laughed.

Not a delicate ladylike laugh that would attract butterflies, but a snorting, stomach-hurting, tears-streaming-down-the-face laugh. As soon as she could get her breath back, Mal said, "I'm glad I'm not the only one without a mental filter," before she burst into a fresh fit of laughter.

"Did I get it all?" she asked Keith a minute later. The family, with a crying Brayden, had packed up and left to go ride the Tilt-A-Whirl. (*Terrible idea,* thought Keith.) They had left Mal with a stack of wet wipes, which Keith was now using to clean lamb juice off his hands.

He looked at Mal's head. It didn't look like she had gotten any of it.

"You missed a spot," he said, poking her head, "here."

"Are you messing with me? I can't see the back of my head, you know."

Keith held out his hand and she gave him the wet wipe. He pulled her head down a little, then gingerly plucked at the mustard in her hair. He felt gooseflesh go up her arm, and he tried not to think about other parts she was feeling tickled. He backed up a bit on the bench. "Got it."

Mal leaned back against the table again and patted her stomach. "With Miss Libby's cooking and all of this cholesterol on a stick, I'm going to have to take one of those hay wagons home. I haven't eaten this much since—well, I don't know since when."

"No dessert?" Keith asked.

Mal looked shocked. "I didn't say I wouldn't eat dessert! I'm just hinting that you're going to have to roll me to the car. Just getting you prepared for that."

Keith laughed. He had a great laugh. The wrinkles around the corners of his eyes came out when he smiled. He was a rugged-looking guy, but when he laughed, he looked like a teddy bear.

"How about a walk around before dessert?" he suggested.

"Yes, absolutely."

They wandered through the crowded fair in silence, Keith waving to people who called his name. Mostly guys in flannel shirts and well-worn cowboy hats, although occasionally a gal in a tight sweater would saunter up and see how Keith was doing. All the traffic had kicked up a lot of mud, and Mal marveled at the variety of sturdy-looking work boots people were wearing—even the little kids, one of whom was struggling with a giant cow (a steer, Keith corrected her) wearing a blue ribbon on its horn. Mal thought if she heard anyone ask if she was Luke's girl again, she was going to stop shaving her legs; mostly, though, she just smiled and said, yes, yes, she was Luke's girl and, no, she wasn't sure when he was getting back to town but probably soon.

There was a moment when Jimmy Dean, off-duty state trooper—and drunk—suggested that Luke was a fool but that Keith was probably keeping her warm, and if he wasn't up to the job, he, Jimmy Dean, would be happy to take over. Keith looked like he was about to sock him in the jaw. But Mal just laughed and said she would rather sleep with the dog.

Jimmy looked up at Keith, surprised. "You still got that old mutt we pulled out of the ditch?"

"He's a good dog," Mal said, defending her new farm ally.

"I don't get you guys. Anyway, I'm going to the beer garden."

Mal was about to suggest dessert (although a beer sounded really good, too) when someone came over and practically knocked Keith to the ground. Mal shrieked and stepped in front of him, only to get mauled by—Katie.

"Sorry," she said, accepting Katie's hand up.

"You didn't do anything," said Keith, glaring at Katie, and absolutely avoiding Mal's gaze. Had she just thrown herself in front of him? "She has this hilarious habit of trying to knock us over."

"One of these days, I'll do it. Preferably in a cow pie."

"You wonder why we still think of you as a little kid," Keith said, pulling one of her pigtails.

"Whatever, listen. Come on over to the beer tent. The music's just starting."

"Oh, I don't think——" Keith began, just as Mal said, "Oh! Dancing!"

"OK, let's go."

The beer tent catered to the new younger, hipper fairgoers, and was not so much a tent as a set of arbors arranged in a large square and covered in white fairy lights. The kegs were more or less covered on one end by a large white tent, but the rest of the area was open to the sky. The space in the middle was dominated by a wooden dance floor. Situated right next to the beer part of the beer tent was a small raised stage where the band played. Keith waved to his old classmate Dylan, one of the fiddlers, who acknowledged him with a wave of his bow.

Katie led them over to a crowd of people standing with easy access to the kegs. Looked like her friends from high school.

Keith couldn't keep their names straight——Beth maybe was the blonde. And one of the guys was probably Trevor. He had no idea who the brunette was, but she looked a little familiar. Jill? Brittany? Good chance it was a Brittany.

Keith stopped worrying about it when someone handed him a beer.

"Next round's on you, old man," said one of the guys. That one was Trevor, he remembered. Luke had told him something about catching Trevor and Katie making out in a car—he knew he didn't like Trevor. Katie was definitely a little tipsy and he didn't like the way Trevor kept putting his arm around her to steady her. Then he saw Chase standing behind them, shooting daggers into the back of Trevor's head. Chase had big-brother duty tonight.

"So how's babysitting?" Chase asked.

"Huh?"

"Katie said you were in charge of Mal today. Is she wearing you out?"

He thought of Mal's eyes lighting up as she took in the festival,

Mal doubled over in laughter. Mal eating the pickle on a stick. "She's OK. I think I've lost her though."

Just then, Keith caught sight of her. She was spinning on the dance floor with Mac MacDonald, who owned the farm up the road.

"The old geezer probably never danced with such a pretty girl in his life," Chase said with a smile.

"She's all right," Keith mumbled. *She's beautiful.*

"Whatever," Chase said, taking a swig of his beer.

Jill or Brittany sidled up to him. "Hey, Katie's big brother, remember me?"

"Uh, sure."

Jill or Brittany put her hand on Keith's arm and it took all he had not to pull away.

"I bet you haven't seen me since your daddy gave me riding lessons when I was a little girl."

She leaned into him, put her hand on his chest.

Keith tried to back away without actually moving.

Her breath smelled like beer. "I'm all grown up now," she breathed into his face. "I'm an excellent rider."

"Jesus, girl," said Chase, laughing. "Leave the poor guy alone."

"Is that what you want, Keith? You want me to leave you alone?" She ran her hand down to the waist of his jeans.

Just then Mal came spinning off the dance floor. "Man, that old guy can dance." She grabbed Keith's beer cup and drained it. "That's pretty good. Hey, I'm Mal," she said to Jill or Brittany.

"I'm Jill. You must be Luke's fiancée," she said, meaning, "Why are you drinking my man's beer?"

Mal looked at Keith, who was trying to project his most desperate get-me-out-of-here face while still maintaining a polite façade. She took pity and grabbed his hand. "Come on, let's dance."

"No, wait, I don't—"

Whatever he was about to say got lost in the crush of hoots and applause as the band started a fast one. Everyone spilled onto the dance floor and he was pressed up against Mal, who was clapping and twirling like a pro.

"What were you saying?" Mal shouted above the noise, a huge happy grin plastered on her face.

"I don't dance!"

"I can see that! Here, give me your hands." She grabbed his hands and started spinning under his arms, shaking him back and forth like you would with a toddler. It was pretty humiliating, but she was grinning up at him, and he thought probably any humiliation was worth that.

"See, you're dancing!"

He laughed, and because it felt so great to be out there in a crowd of people dancing with a beautiful girl, he picked her up and swung her around.

When he put her down, she was holding on to his arms and looking up at him with a stunned expression. The song ended, and the band started a slow number. Couples formed around them, pairing off and melting into one, swaying to the music under the humid night sky. "Drink?" Keith said.

Chapter 11

Four beers and a deep-fried cheesecake on a stick later, Mal was drunk. She leaned her forehead against the closed window in the backseat of Chase's car, trying to focus on the lyrics of the country song on the radio. Something about a cheating heart. The two-door sports car had a tiny backseat, and it was a very bumpy ride. Too bumpy for her bumpy stomach.

"You OK back there?" Keith asked, more or less without slurring, from the front passenger seat. He seemed to have had two beers to her every one. But he was a big guy. A big, strong, hairy guy. He could lift hay bales. He could drink twelve beers. Was that four times two, she wondered?

"What?" Keith turned around, blinked, then turned quickly back to the front.

Chase rolled down the front windows. "Please don't throw up on my leather seats."

"If you had a truck like a normal person, I could throw up anywhere." Keith definitely slurred that time. "Wait, that's not—"

Finishing that sentence seemed to be too much work, so he let his head drop back on the headrest. "Hey, thanks for the ride, man."

"No problem. You are definitely not in a state to drive."

"I know, and after . . ." Keith's words trailed off and he stared out the open window.

Mal closed her eyes. The backseat spun for a moment, like she was still on the dance floor. Michael never let her dance, she thought. Then everything faded away.

* * *

When Chase pulled into the Carson's driveway, Keith motioned for him to stop at the big house. "I'll make sure Mal gets in OK. I can walk home."

"You sure?"

"Chase, it's like——" He waved in the general direction of the house. "I can do it."

"Do you have house keys?"

Keith gave him what he hoped was a withering look, then spilled out of the car. He pulled the seat forward and reached back to help Mal out. She was out cold. "Mal," he whispered, not wanting to disturb her——she looked sweet and peaceful and quiet——but also not wanting her to sleep in the car. With Chase. *"Mal,"* he whispered even louder. Chase gave him a look, then reached back and pinched Mal on her thigh. She jumped up, hit her head on the roof, and, groaning, looked around, finally meeting Keith's eyes.

"Hey," she said in a sleepy voice. Damn, it was sexy.

"Come on," he said, "let's go to bed."

"OK," she said, taking his hand. "I'll tell Luke tomorrow." She had some trouble levering herself out of the seat, so Keith gave her hand a gentle tug. At that, she catapulted out of the seat and into Keith's chest, nearly knocking him over. "Whoa," she said. "I'm strong."

Keith closed the car door and waved to Chase. Then he walked, dragging Mal, to the front door, where he reached up and pulled the key out of the loose piece of siding on the right side and inserted it into the lock. As he maneuvered Mal through the doorway, he heard Chase drive away. Mal looked up at him with bleary eyes. "Thank you for bringing me home." She looked around the hall. "Which one is my room again?"

Keith hitched her arm over his shoulder and put his other arm around her waist. He half carried her up the stairs and down the hall. When he got to her room, he tripped over a pair of shoes and pitched forward onto the bed. Moving more quickly than he would have thought possible, he rolled and fell on his back onto the bed, with Mal on top of him. She looked up at him in shock. She was definitely awake now. She looked into his eyes, her brown eyes warm and focused. She raised her hand and brushed his dark hair off his forehead.

"Am I crushing you?" she whispered.

"No, you're OK," he whispered back, his eyes drifting to her lips.

He felt her breath on his mouth as she moved closer. *No*, he thought, but then her lips connected with his and he thought, *Yes*. They were soft and warm and slightly insistent. His hands came up to cup the sides of her face with the intention to push her away—to push *his brother's fiancée* away—but then she gently pushed her tongue into his mouth, and he was lost.

He opened his mouth wider, tilting his head so his tongue could explore her the way she was doing to him. She was a damn good kisser. His hands swept down, across her shoulders, down her sides, past her waist to the soft curves of her butt. He just let his hands run up and down her body, memorizing the shape of her curves beneath his rough hands. Her hands were moving, too, under his shirt to the warm skin of his chest, and he gasped as her hands moved lower, but he didn't want to think, he just wanted to kiss her, so he hitched her up higher on his body and pulled her even closer.

In the back of her mind, Mal knew she should not be doing whatever it was she was doing. But it felt so right and so delicious that she couldn't find the sense to stop. She was kissing Keith. This was no sloppy too-much-beer kiss. They were focused on each other, devouring each other's mouths, and when his hands roamed from her face down her sides, she sighed and let her hands do their own explorations. The skin under his shirt was so warm, taut and smooth and prickly with hair.

Keith ran his hands across her front, cupping her breasts and gently squeezing, and she moaned into his mouth. His hands *were* big, she thought, and strong. She moved her hand over the front of his jeans. He was big all over, she thought, pushing away a vague warning bell in the back of her mind. She reached for the button on his jeans.

And was abruptly dumped on the floor.

"Damn," Keith said, rubbing his face. "God, I'm sorry," he said, reaching down to pick her up off the floor.

She got up on her own and brushed off her ego.

"Keith—" Mal started. Keith shot off the bed and toward the door.

"No, I'm sorry. You're my brother's fiancée. This was a mistake. I've put you in a terrible position."

"It wasn't so terrible," she murmured, looking at the floor.

"Dammit, Mal," he said, and she thought he was going to reach for her again, and she was ready for whatever terrible positions he could come up with.

But he didn't. He shoved his hands in his pockets—a little less room in those jeans now, she observed—then turned and kicked the dresser. "Good night," he said, almost running into the door frame on his way out. "I'm sorry."

"I'm not," she whispered to the closed door. She sat on the edge of the bed, toed off her shoes. *Crap,* she thought. *Just, crap.*

Chapter 12

Mal woke up with a headache.

It was much worse when she opened her eyes, what with the sun streaming in through the window, all warm and friendly and welcoming. Stupid sun. She silently cursed whoever had let her fall asleep with the curtains open.

Then she remembered the last person in her room the night before. Keith. With the hands and the tongue and the jeans.

That made her headache even worse.

She should feel terrible, she thought. She should regret putting him in the terrible position (not *so* terrible, she remembered), of thinking he was making her cheat on his own brother. But she wasn't engaged to Luke. She was free to kiss whichever scowling cowboy she wanted to.

Of course, Keith didn't know that. Neither did any of the Carson family. Except Luke. *That's it,* she decided, reaching blindly for her cell phone. *Luke needs to come home, and we need to clear this up.* Every day she spent in Hollow Bend, she got deeper and deeper into their lives. She practically had a job interview at Dr. Monroe's.

It would be nice to work, though. She didn't mind the hard, physical labor of the farm (although her back sort of minded), but she loved numbers.

She had dropped out of school just three credits shy of her accounting degree. She had wanted to take the CPA exam and work for nonprofit organizations. Her vision was to work cheap; Michael would be a doctor, so they would be able to afford it. She wanted to work cheap and work for good causes, groups that wouldn't be able to hire a good accountant normally. Women's shelters, libraries, garden clubs—whatever. Anyone who was doing something they loved, something good.

But Michael's residency had taken them from Connecticut to Maryland, and he wanted to get married before he left. She didn't want to break up with him, not really, so she agreed. They went to the justice of the peace, signed some papers, and that was it.

Then Michael said he didn't like the idea of his wife being so far away, especially during their first year as husband and wife. He promised when he was a rich doctor, she could go back to school and study whatever she wanted. And he needed her. He was so busy, he was becoming really scatterbrained. He would forget to eat if it wasn't for her.

So they moved to Maryland. She worked, doing the books for a local car dealership. Not exactly what she'd envisioned, but even though she reported to a real accountant, the books were complicated enough to keep her interested. She supported them while Michael worked his crazy hospital hours in pediatric oncology.

Then the work he did started receiving attention, which he deserved. He was so dedicated, so passionate about his work. He would come home from a shift on the pediatric ward exhausted and heartbroken that he couldn't do more, that he couldn't just fix the problem like a broken bone and be done. She loved him so much then; she was seeing the side of Michael she liked the best. Not the side that was in pain, but the side that had compassion and drive. That, she had thought, was why they made such a good couple.

She wasn't entirely sure how the decision for her to stop working came about. Michael was rising in the ranks, and he wanted to impress the administration and the board. And the best way for him to get to the top was for both of them to be working toward that goal. Anyway, he was curing cancer; Mal was balancing the books for a low-rent car dealership. There was no contest, really.

So she quit her job, set up the house. She tried to manage the cooking and cleaning with as much enthusiasm as she managed accounts, but it wasn't the same. She missed numbers. Michael suggested she start counting calories.

She shook her head, remembering the years of charity committees and girls' nights out. Of frying her hair blond and the horrific realization of what a Brazilian bikini wax actually *was*. Of shopping with the other doctors' wives, how it didn't seem right to spend thousands of dollars on clothes she would only wear once, but how Michael insisted, saying that they could afford it.

Michael thought she could channel her do-gooder energies into charity work, so she sat on committees, planned luncheons, bid on things she didn't need at charity auctions. This was not what she wanted to do. So when she contacted a battered women's shelter about doing a fund-raiser for them, and they told her they would love the money, but what they really needed was for someone to help write grants and manage the donations they received every year, Mal jumped at the chance. She quit her committees and dug into the shelter's books.

They were a mess. The director had been doing just enough to keep them afloat. Mal saw that jumble of mismatched spreadsheets, disorganized invoices, uneven balances, and she almost started drooling. She could help with this. This, she could fix.

And she did. Michael was not thrilled that she'd quit her committee work—if the other wives liked her, they would be invited more places and he would get ahead even faster. But if this was what she really wanted to do, he would just work that much harder. He would work hard for both of them.

Mal was too happy with her work to feel guilty. She spent six months straightening out the old books, then streamlining the shelter's bookkeeping procedures so that they were simpler to follow. She trained a few of the residents on how to receive the invoices and log them into the system so she could pay the bills. She even started working on a grant from the state for a small computer center where she could train more residents, help them with resumes.

Then the center was audited. Somehow the fact that she wasn't an official CPA received some attention, and the IRS came in, went over everything with a fine-toothed comb. The books were perfect; she was sure of it. But the grant-making bodies were not satisfied with her qualifications and other donors got cold feet.

The shelter was closed six months later.

Mal's heart was broken. The director was shattered, and the residents—they quickly scattered. Mal hoped they'd landed on their feet, but she wasn't an idiot.

Then she found out who had alerted the state to her lack of qualifications.

Michael said he'd done it for her own good, that he wasn't sure if she was qualified to take on such a big project, and obviously she wasn't. "Look what happened when the authorities found out what you were doing."

"Women are homeless because of you," she said, "women who were abused and who had no other options."

"There's no need for histrionics," he said. "And now you have more time for committee work, which is much more effective anyway. Bill—you know, Dr. Ashton-Pierce—was telling me his wife is working on something new, something with animals or kids . . ."

Mal felt a gentle pressure on her knee and started. Peanut was resting his head on her lap, looking up at her with those brown puppy-dog eyes. His tongue lolled out when she looked at him.

"You big lump," she said, bending down to scratch his head. Peanut took that as an invitation and jumped on the bed, licking her face, then curling into a ball at her side.

"Are you comfortable? Good," said Mal as she tried to hang on to the end of the bed. Then she gave up the struggle, leaned against Peanut, and tried to go back to sleep.

Except she couldn't. Her head hurt, and she couldn't stop thinking about what she was going to say when she went downstairs. She had jumped on Keith last night. True, he had jumped back, at least she thought he had—her memory was a little fuzzy. Whatever he had done, she'd liked it. She liked kissing him.

But he still thought she was engaged to his brother. So he was probably feeling pretty bad right now. That was not the way she wanted him to feel about kissing her. She wasn't sure why it mattered, exactly. Once Luke got back, she'd tell them all the truth and she'd go. Even if Keith had no problem kissing attached women (which she doubted), he probably didn't have a great fondness for kissing liars.

That's what she was. She was weak, she was a doormat, and now she was a liar. "I'm really building up quite a resume," she said into Peanut's head.

He licked her nose.

She had read a book once where the main character could just close her eyes and will herself to sleep, and, boom, she slept. "Go to sleep," Mal intoned in what she hoped was a convincing voice. "Peanut, knock it off," she said as Peanut rolled over onto her. So she did what she used to do with Michael when she couldn't sleep. She lay as still as possible, staring at the ceiling. There were forty-three small cracks in the ceiling, and she was awake.

She had just about decided to bite the bullet and go down for breakfast when her phone rang. *Good,* she thought. *It's Luke.* Then suddenly that didn't seem so good. Did she tell him she'd kissed his brother? Why should it matter to him? But the need to find out when the hell he was coming to get her won out, and she snapped open the phone.

"Luke, please, I'm begging you——"

"Who's Luke?"

Not Luke, she thought. *Michael.*

"Michael?" she whispered, hoping maybe she was mistaken.

"Yes, Mallory, it's your husband. Have you forgotten me so soon?"

"How did you get this number?" Her heart was beating faster, her hands sweating. She didn't know she was shaking until Peanut whimpered, put his head on her lap, and stilled her.

"Mallory, you were always so stupid with money. You put the cell phone purchase on my credit card. I just looked at the statement, and there it was."

"Oh." That was a stupid thing to do. She *was* stupid.

"What do you want?"

"Well, first of all, I want to know why you insisted on running away. Honestly, you're like a child trying to avoid punishment. It's a little ridiculous, and, frankly, a little embarrassing. Do you know what people are saying about you here? About us?"

"I'm sorry, Michael. I just couldn't . . ." She couldn't say what she couldn't. She couldn't talk to him; somehow, when she tried, he just sucked all the words right back, leaving none for her.

"I gave you your separation, I gave you everything you ever wanted. Mallory, if we had a problem, we could have talked about it. I would have sat down with you, let you explain everything, and we would have found a solution. But every time I ask you what's wrong—and I have been asking that a lot lately, Mallory—you have nothing to say. I don't understand. How can I make it right if I don't know what's wrong?"

Everything is wrong, she wanted to shout. *You belittle me, you control me, you bully me, and when I try to tell you how I feel, you explain it all away like it's my fault! Like I'm being paranoid! You*

say you don't want to be with me, but you won't let me go! She was
gripping the phone hard, pressing it tight to her ear. And she was
moving her mouth, but nothing was coming out. She couldn't figure
out how to say anything to him. Frustration, rage bubbled up inside
of her and spilled out in hot tears down her cheeks. Why couldn't
she talk to him? Maybe he was right; maybe if she couldn't articulate
it, it was nothing.

"The women's shelter," she said. That, she knew, was something
bad he'd done. She was mad about that.

"Mallory, that was ages ago. Anyway, Bunny is fixing your mistake. She's organizing a fund-raiser to get a new shelter built, state
of the art."

"My mistake?"

"Yes, Mallory, we went over this. If you hadn't bitten off more than
you could chew, the shelter wouldn't have been shut down. Anyway,
that's the past. Bunny said you just needed a break, that it was intense
having such a go-getter husband. Is that the problem, Mallory?"

If she said yes, maybe this conversation would go away. He was
going to believe that it was all her fault anyway, that none of the
flaws were his. Why not just let him have the satisfaction of being
right? Maybe then she would get the divorce, not just a separation.

"Mallory, are you there?"

"Yes."

"I don't understand why you're not answering me."

"I don't know what to say, Michael."

"Well, I have to say something to you, and it's going to be very
painful. I would have preferred to say this in person, but since you
refuse to deal with our marriage head-on, I'm forced to do it this way."

Mal braced herself.

"It's not working, Mallory. You're not communicating with me,
you're shutting me out. Bunny says that's not good for me, and that
it's affecting my career."

Bunny, she thought. *Why does he keep talking about Bunny?*

"I want to go ahead and finalize our divorce. I know I told you
the separation was just a trial, but I can't stay married to someone
who would abandon me like this."

Mal let out a laugh, tears of relief streaming down her face. He
was calling her to get a divorce.

"I know this is a shock, but I can't help feeling it's what you wanted all along. I thought we were a team, that we were focused on the same goal. But lately, I don't know, Mal. What happened to that vivacious girl I married?"

Vivacious? Mal didn't remember ever being exactly vivacious. "It's hard being married to you, Michael. You're very demanding."

Michael sighed. "I don't think I ask for anything out of the ordinary. Just a little common sense and a little support from my *wife*. It shouldn't be that hard if you love me."

Mal felt her whole body wilt. She put her hand on Peanut's head and petted behind his ears. She didn't know how to respond to him. She knew what she wanted to say—that she didn't love him, that she wasn't sure she had ever loved him, that he had done a pretty good job of convincing her of who she was and what she wanted, but that he had it all wrong. He didn't know her at all. He didn't love her, either.

Of course, Michael's sleeping with other women hadn't helped.

"I'm sorry, Michael. I think this is for the best."

"Good. I had the papers drawn up. Now, even though I made all the money, I'll do my best to give you something you can live on."

I can make my own money, she thought. But then, she revised: *I can make my own money later. Let me get some of his first. I earned it.*

"Thanks."

"I'll give you a call later in the week when everything is in order. You will still have this phone number, won't you? You won't throw it out and get another one?"

"No, Michael, I'll keep this phone."

"Good, because that's just the sort of thing I would expect you to do." She heard him take a deep breath. "Mallory, I can't tell you how great it feels for us to talk like this. It will be good to see you again."

"Sure." It will be good to sign those divorce papers.

"A little enthusiasm, Mal. *You're* the one who ran away from *me*, remember? You're lucky I'm even considering giving you anything in this divorce. I'm way too forgiving of you, Mal."

"I'm very grateful, Michael."

"Well, I should go. I told Bunny I'd go to her tennis tournament. Her husband is working so much, and I know what it's like to have a spouse who doesn't support you."

Mal hit her head against the pillow. "Well, you won't have to worry about that for long."

Michael laughed. "I won't miss that sense of humor, but it has been good to talk to you. I'll call you later. Don't lose your phone."

Mal only just resisted the urge to throw her phone across the room—it wouldn't do to prove Michael right by calling him with a new phone number. Instead, she flopped back on the bed, threw her arm up over her eyes, and cried. She tried to be quiet about it, but little sobs kept escaping.

She couldn't stop crying. She was getting divorced—the best news she had heard since, well, since Michael had agreed to a separation. But Michael was the same Michael—not understanding her, not seeing her at all, not getting why her square peg couldn't fit into his round hole. She laughed a little at the unfortunate metaphor. Then she cried again—he wouldn't miss her sense of humor. God, what a dick. Why the hell had she put up with him for so long?

Because she'd believed him. She'd believed everything he said about her—that she was fat, that she was clumsy, that she was stupid. She'd believed him when he told her that she was lucky to be with someone as successful and as driven as him, someone who didn't mind that his wife was a complete failure. He would just have to be successful enough for both of them.

Peanut whined and put his head on her stomach. She leaned up on her elbows, and he lifted those big doggy eyes to her. "I was a real idiot, Peanut." Peanut whined again. "No, listen, it's okay. Because I'm done with Michael now. And now I can do whatever I want. I can go anywhere. I've never been so happy."

And she broke down in tears.

Libby smacked Keith on his rear and told him to sit down and use utensils like a human being.

"I'm in a hurry," he said around a mouthful of toast.

"That's no reason to eat like an animal. Sit. Or no more food."

He sat down with the rest of the family in a huff, but the huff exacerbated his headache, so he slowed down, chewed, swallowed, and reached for the coffee.

He was in a hurry, that was true. He had woken up late, and with a raging headache. Then he had remembered why he had been up so late and why his head hurt so badly. Beer tent. Dancing. Mal.

He shouldn't have kissed her. If he thought back to last night, which he tried not to do at the family breakfast table, he could remember that really, it was Mal who'd started it. She'd kissed him first. But it didn't seem very gentlemanly of him to admit that. Anyway, *she* was the one who was engaged, not him. So what if he'd been looking at her curves since she got here. So what if he'd kissed her back because he had been dreaming of doing that for the past few days.

He heard the water shut off upstairs, which meant Mal was getting out of the shower. Which meant she was wet. Which also meant she would be down soon. Keith wanted to be long gone when she got here.

"You still repairing fences today?" he asked Chase, sitting across the table next to a very bleary-looking Katie.

"Don't talk with your mouth full," said Libby.

"Yeah, there's just a big post down on the far end of the property. Shouldn't take long," Chase said. With his mouth full.

"I'll help you."

"I think Cal wants to——"

"Let him help you," Cal grumbled. "I'm sick of your jabbering. If I wanted to talk while I worked, I'd join a damn quilting bee."

"Have some more coffee, Cal."

"That'll help." Katie snorted. She was looking a little green this morning. In fact, Keith thought she was wearing the same shirt she had been wearing last night at the fair. He shook his head. *Don't even think about that.*

"Who wants more eggs?" Libby asked. Every hand went up, and she started over to the table with the pan, dishing out eggs to her surly, hung over family.

"Morning."

Damn, Keith thought. Mal stood in the doorway to the kitchen, wearing those same old jeans and T-shirt. Her hair was pulled back in a ponytail, but he could see that it was still wet. She had dark circles under her eyes. She didn't look as bad as he felt, but close. He shouldn't have asked for more eggs.

"Morning, sweetheart," Libby said. "Come on over and get some eggs. There's plenty. Coffee's in the pot."

Mal looked at the coffeepot, then at Libby and the Carsons, all more or less silently shoveling breakfast into their faces. And she burst into tears.

Keith jumped out of his seat, and the others looked up at him. In that instant, they all noticed Mal crying. Keith sat back down. *Leave her be,* he thought.

"I'm sorry," she said to the table of staring faces. "I thought I could . . . But I just . . . And then Luke said . . . I'm sorry. I can't." She turned to go, but Peanut was standing behind her and she tried to stop herself from stepping on him. But she ended up going face-first onto the floor.

Keith was really on his feet this time, and so was everyone else at the table. He reached her first, pulled her up to a seated position. Now she was laughing.

"Jeez, Mal."

She put her hand on his arm, steadying herself as she caught her breath. He looked over his shoulder at his family.

Katie shrugged. "She's losing it."

Libby shooed them all out of the way and guided Mal to her feet. Then Libby did what she did best, what Keith always remembered her doing even when he thought he was too big or too tough for it. She folded her arms around Mal and pulled her head down to her shoulder, and gently rocked back and forth. Mal sobbed a little more, then took a deep, shuddering sigh and lifted her head up.

"Come have some breakfast," Libby said. "You'll feel better with some food in you. Then you can tell us all about it."

Mal nodded, then let Miss Libby lead her into the kitchen by the hand. She shooed Keith out of his seat and sat Mal down.

Mal started talking before she took her first mouthful of food.

"I'm not engaged to Luke. I'm already married."

Chapter 13

"I don't like being kicked out of my own house," Cal muttered as he saddled his horse. The big black mare snorted and shifted, so Cal slowed down, patted her gently.

"Did you want to sit in there with those waterworks? I don't think I've ever seen someone cry so much before." Chase was gathering supplies, throwing tools and hinges into a big white plastic bucket. "Keith, are you ready to go or what?"

Keith was already sitting on his horse, which was walking in agitated little circles right outside the barn.

"Son, you better calm down or that horse is gonna throw you."

Duchess hadn't thrown him in the sixteen years he'd known her, and he'd met her when Dr. Monroe delivered her right in that barn. Duchess had made him want to be a vet. Duchess wouldn't mind a little frustration over lusting after a woman you'd thought was your brother's fiancée but turned out to be someone else's wife.

"Are we fixing those fences or what?"

"Keith, there's really not that much left. I just have to check that outer perimeter by the creek, but I told you, I think it'll hold up another winter." Chase was mounting his horse, Bruiser, and coming out of the barn, supplies in tow.

Keith didn't say anything, just leaned forward to try to soothe Duchess. He did need to calm down.

"But if you need to ride, don't let me stop you."

"Why would I need to ride?"

"You seem a little agitated."

Keith didn't say anything, just looked toward the house.

"She really had us all fooled, didn't she?" Chase said. "I mean, I wasn't real convinced that Luke was that serious about her, but I never would have guessed that she's already married."

"Are you boys done jabbering, or should I send the staff out to fix the fence?"

Keith turned Duchess and followed Chase and his father out to mend the broken fence.

Mal was sitting in the kitchen, clutching a mug of coffee like a lifeline. Libby had shooed the men out, but Katie sat next to her at the table, half pissed at having been duped, half curious at Mal's story. So Mal started at the beginning. How she met Michael in college. How she helped him pass history. How, when her parents were killed in a car crash, he took care of her.

"Oh, bless your heart, you were all alone," said Libby, reaching across the table for her hand.

Michael had been wonderful then. When the RA came up to give her the news, she was inconsolable. She tried to get Mal to the counseling center, or at least to talk to the house mother, but the only one who got her to calm down was Michael. He came into her room and held her. She vaguely remembered hearing him talk to the others who came through, asking her roommate to crash elsewhere, sending the RA out for food. That night he changed her into her pajamas and tucked her into bed like she was a child. She didn't want him to leave. So he kicked off his shoes and climbed into bed with her, even though it was against dorm rules for him to spend the night. He kissed her forehead, held her close, and said, "I'll take care of you now."

She had liked him pretty well before, but that was when she fell in love with him.

"He did everything for me. He arranged for me to defer my exams, he made me eat. I'm pretty sure he even showered me a few times. I felt like I owed him a debt of gratitude for how truly wonderful he was then."

Libby shook her head. "He was just doing what any man should do in a crisis. Taking care of his partner. There's no debt to be repaid. You would have done the same for him."

Mal looked up at her. How could she explain the way Michael

made her repay that debt? How his expectations of gratitude and entitlement made him unbearable?

So she told them the rest. How they moved to Maryland even though she wasn't finished with school, and how he insisted they get married first. How he sold her parents' house to finance the move. How she worked, and then she stopped working. How she dyed her hair, shopped, joined committees.

"I did everything he asked, but it was never right. I joined a book club at the library, and he said that was beneath me, that he made enough money so I didn't need to get my books for free. He would buy me all the books I wanted. He wouldn't even let me return the book," Mal said with a sad laugh.

"Are you kidding me? Why didn't you just return the book? While he was at work or something?" Katie was giving her an incredulous look. She wasn't sure if it was directed at her or Michael.

"If I 'defied' him—his word—he would never let me forget it. He wouldn't let me forget how he worked hard, how he was the only one who brought in money——"

"He wouldn't let you work!"

"——and then he would remember some other stupid thing I did, and how I had let myself go since we got married. It just became easier to do what he wanted. I think that book is still in the house somewhere. I should go return it."

"He sounds like a toad," Katie said.

"Don't insult toads, dear," said Libby.

"I don't understand," Katie said, leaning back to reach for a biscuit from the basket on the counter. "I mean, look at you. You're funny, you're hot, you're clearly not an idiot—maybe with horses, but you seem to have tamed Peanut, so that says something."

"Thanks," said Mal, patting Peanut's head. He had been sitting with his head on her lap for the past hour while Mal spilled her guts. *What a loyal friend,* she thought. Or maybe it's the bacon.

"But that's just it. You stood up to me just fine when I was giving you shit about letting Bob out."

"Language, Katie," said Libby, refilling Mal's coffee cup.

"Sorry. And Keith, he tried to take care of your dog problem, and you went behind his back and fixed it yourself. I don't understand how you can stand up for yourself here, but you couldn't even tell your husband you wanted to return a library book."

"I don't know," Mal said, fingering Peanut's collar. "I don't. I wish I could figure it out. Maybe it's because here, I don't already know you, and I figured you already had a pretty bad opinion of me, so I had nothing to lose." And none of the Carsons had Michael's temper, she thought, flinching involuntarily.

"Why on earth would we have a bad opinion of you?" asked Libby.

"Because she showed up out of nowhere, allegedly engaged, and then she let the horse out," replied Katie, helpfully. "And she doesn't own work boots."

Mal tried to laugh, but it came out as a halfhearted snort. "Anyway, I knew I wouldn't be staying here. I knew I would never see you guys again. But I had to live with Michael, and it seemed easier just to make the way as smooth as possible."

"By giving up yourself," said Libby, stroking Mal's hair. "That's not a marriage, sweetheart. I don't know what that is, but it's no way to live."

"So are you going back or what?"

Mal looked at Katie. "I should, I guess. But not to stay. Michael's agreed to the divorce. I'm letting him think it was his idea. He's not too thrilled I ran off. I made him look bad."

Libby patted Mal's hand. "Maybe it's for the best. Some people are just not cut out for marriage." Mal wasn't sure if she meant her or Michael. She stirred a little sugar in her coffee.

"I still don't get it, Mal. But if you're unhappy with him, you should go back, kick his ass, and move on." Katie rose from her seat and reached for her jacket on the peg next to the door. "Now this has been real enlightening, but as my dear kind father likes to say, it's time to quit jabbering and get to work."

She turned before she went out the door. "I'm real sorry that you've had a rough time, Mal. I like you. I think you would have been good for Luke." Then she headed out to the barn.

"Luke," Mal said, groaning. "Luke's gonna kill me. I promised I wouldn't tell you guys and that I would stay put until he got back."

"Well, you can't sit around forever."

"Although I will sit around until he can give me a ride back to DC. I should probably go get some more clothes, too." Mal could not think of a single thing that she wanted from Michael's house, but a second pair of jeans was probably in order.

"I tell you, that boy wears me out. I don't understand why girls act so daffy around him. Anyway, I think Katie's right, you'd be good for him. You should marry him."

"Luke's a good friend," said Mal. "But he's definitely just a friend."

Luke was a handsome guy, all right. Strong jaw, piercing eyes, the whole thing. But on the whole, Mal found she preferred guys who were a little rougher, whose haircut maybe wasn't so au courant, whose clothes were a little more careless. Guys with green eyes and dirty jeans who made her feel like they wanted to spend time with her, answering her dingbat questions about farm animals. Guys who kissed her back.

"Ugh," groaned Mal, planting her forehead on the table. Her headache was definitely back. And she was falling for Keith.

She should probably go to DC to get that divorce.

Chapter 14

The fencing took much less time than they thought it would, especially when Katie rode up, making four people to do a two-person job. Keith didn't think she was really interested in the fence, though (although to be fair, neither was he); she just wanted to talk about Mal.

"Her husband's a real jerk," Katie said. "It sounds like he made her feel like shit all the time." She relished the freedom of speech working away from the house gave her.

"So he abused her?" Chase asked, tipping his hat up to look at Katie.

Keith slammed the hammer down wrong, bending a nail. He cursed softly and started digging it out.

"Maybe. I mean, I don't think he hit her or anything. Keith, what the hell are you doing to that board?"

"Nothing. Fixing it."

"Give it to me," she said, taking the hammer. She brought the claw down hard and sharp and pulled the nail right out. She was always better at that than Keith was. "Even after they were separated, he still made her do his laundry. I guess you have to be pretty worn down to put up with crap like that. I don't really get it, but finally she couldn't take it anymore, so she ran off with Luke."

"Luke does have a talent for getting girls to run off with him," said Chase. He started throwing the tools and bent nails into the bucket.

"Yeah, but this is different. I mean, she doesn't have that gaga face that girls get when they talk about Luke. And thank goodness, because I have to sit across the table from her when I eat. I think she knew Luke from town or something. Just friends."

"He also has a talent for being in the right place at the right time."

"So, what, she just ran away? From her husband? And her family?"

Katie looked at Keith sharply. "She doesn't have a family. Just an asshole husband. You don't know what it's like for her, you don't know why she left."

"Neither do you! You just said you don't get it!"

"Quit shouting at me, Keith! I said I don't get it, because why would someone let her husband beat her down like that! I don't get why she didn't stand up for herself! I'm not saying it didn't happen!"

"But why is she still here? What does she want from us?"

"She doesn't want anything, Keith. She has her space, Luke's gonna come get her, then she's going to get a divorce. Then she'll be gone. What do you think, that she's a spy? Coming to steal our secrets? How to run a horse farm into the ground with apathy and a complete resistance to change?"

"Watch it," Chase warned as Cal approached.

"When you run a horse farm, you can do whatever you damn well please with it," said Cal, stepping toe-to-toe with his daughter. "Stay out of my business."

"Stay out of your business? That's fine, until you need help, then it's 'that girl doesn't pull her weight around here.' I don't want to run a horse farm, Dad, I want to run *this* one."

"Well, I'm still running it, so I guess you'll have to wait until I'm dead."

"If you call this running it! Do you know why it takes Keith so long to do the books? Because *we don't make any money.* If you would just take a few chances——"

"Chances cost money, which you just said we don't have."

"Dad, there are ways to make changes! You can get investors, or a loan. Chase said he would—"

"I'm not taking anybody's money to run my farm! The Carsons have always done for themselves!" Cal was turning red. Katie had pushed him too hard. As usual. "If you want to take money from strangers, go ahead, but like I said, you'll have to wait until I'm dead." He turned on his heel, spat on the ground, and started walking his horse back toward the house.

Chase came up behind Katie and put a hand on her shoulder. She shook it off, kicked the dirt. "Even when he's dead I won't get a chance. He's going to leave the farm to you," she said, pointing her hammer at Keith.

"Or Luke." Keith shrugged.

"That will be the ultimate insult. Leaving the farm to a guy who hasn't spent two weeks here in his entire adult life."

"Maybe Luke'll let you run it," Chase said. Katie punched him in the arm. But she smiled when she did it. He threw his arm around her shoulders and all three followed Cal's path back to the barn.

Keith was putting up the tools in the work shed when he felt someone come up behind him.

"Hi," Mal said. He didn't turn around. Maybe if he ignored her, she would leave him alone.

He heard her take a deep breath, let it out. "I'm sorry. I'm sorry for kissing you like that last night."

That got him whirling around to face her. "What?"

She stepped back a little. "I'm sorry for kissing you. I know it was wrong because I'm married, but I just—"

"You didn't kiss me. I kissed you. Which I wouldn't have done if I had known you were married."

"Technically, I'm separated. Divorce imminent."

Keith raised his eyebrow.

"Anyway, are we really going to argue over who kissed who first? Even though it was clearly me and you're completely delusional if you think you're the one who started it."

"You're memory's fuzzy, Mal."

"No! I know I'm right. You tripped, then I fell on top of you, then you stared into my eyes and brushed back my hair—"

"And then I kissed you," Keith said softly.

"No, then I kissed you," Mal replied, taking a step forward. He looked into her brown eyes, seeing, what? Regret? He wanted to brush back her hair and kiss her again.

"You're married," he whispered.

"I'm very sorry about that," Mal said, not breaking from his gaze. "On many levels."

They stood there for a long moment, staring. "Keith—"

"No, forget it. It's fine. You successfully took advantage of the hillbillies. You win."

"Do you think that's what I wanted? I wanted to tell you the truth, it was Luke—"

"Yeah, yeah, Luke. You seem to be pretty good at getting Luke to do what you want. But that only works up to a point, right? So you got your way with one brother, why not try the other one?"

Mal flinched, then said quietly, "Is that what you think of me?"

Seeing her flinch like that, as if he'd hit her, as if he was the one who'd hurt her, made his gut drop. He wasn't the bad guy here, so why did he feel like one? "What the hell am I supposed to think? You show up out of nowhere, then you tell me you're *married* and you're just here for, for what?" He knew he was yelling; he should stop yelling. "Is this a damn vacation for you? Just a little trip until you go back to your real life? Why are you here, Mal?"

Even though he couldn't control himself, his anger seemed to shift something in her. She looked at him solidly. "I'm here to muck out the stalls."

"Oh! Thank goodness you're here!" Billie Monroe stood in the doorway of the shed, looking flushed and out of breath.

"What's wrong? Is Dr. Monroe all right?" Keith started to brush past Mal.

"No. I mean, yes, he's fine. We're fine. I need Mal," she said, reaching out her hand. Mal took it and stepped forward out of the barn. "At the fair, when we were in the wagon thingy? You said you were a bookkeeper?"

"Yes," Mal said, hesitating. "I was a bookkeeper."

"We need you. *I* need you. Our bookkeeper quit to go have a baby."

"Linda?" Keith asked. "Linda had her baby months ago."

"I know. I've been doing the books for almost a year now. I'm not an accountant, Mal. I hate math. Guts and blood, fine, yes, no problem. But numbers give me hives."

"Why do you need me now?"

"Because I'm going crazy! Vendors are calling looking for their checks, but I swear I sent them. And this afternoon, I was looking for an invoice under the desk and a pile of papers just fell on my head. It's a health hazard! And I'm hung over from the beer garden and my dad won't hire someone else in case Linda wants to come back—even though she said she wouldn't! She quit a year ago! And I remembered what you said about being a bookkeeper. And I think maybe you are a nice person, and you like to help out people who are going crazy, right? So will you? Will you help me, Mal?"

"Help you organize your books?"

"Yes, please."

"Will there be filing?"

Billie looked sheepish. "There might be a little filing. But I'll help with that part!"

"Oh, no way. That's all mine," Mal said, her face lighting up. She turned to Keith. "Do you think that's OK? If I go with her?"

The way she was looking at him—it made something happen in his chest. Her smile was wide and real, it reached all the way to her bright eyes. Paperwork, he told himself. She's looking at you like that because of paperwork.

"Yeah, we don't need you here."

The second he said it, he wanted to take it back. He didn't mean it like that. He meant it like, they could handle the chores on their own, the way they had been doing for years.

She looked crestfallen all the same, and that look was a punch in his gut. His poor guts were taking a beating from this woman. But they didn't need her; not to be cruel, just a fact.

Anyway, she was married. Not that they would need her if she wasn't. They didn't need her. *He* didn't need her at all.

"I'll have her back by supper. You can tell Libby I swear it," Billie said, not feeling the tension radiating between the two people standing on opposite sides of the shed door. She grabbed Mal's hand again, practically pulling her toward her waiting truck. Mal climbed in, put on her seat belt, and didn't look back as Billie pulled out, kicking up dirt as she sped down the road.

Chapter 15

"You OK?" Billie asked. Mal was looking silently out the window. "Was there something else you should be doing? I didn't mean to take you away from—"

"No, that's OK. Keith was right. They don't need me there. I don't know anything about horses anyway. I'm sort of a pain in the butt to them."

Billie laughed. "I don't think that's it."

"What?"

"Nothing. Look, are you sure about this? It's a lot of mess. Papers everywhere, I'm telling you. Although I should also warn you that if you say no, I've got a shotgun."

Mal smiled. She must really be getting used to Kentucky if shotgun jokes were funny to her. She shouldn't do that, though. There was no sense getting used to being here, since she was going to leave as soon as Luke came back. "I'm sure. I seriously do love filing. It's a sickness."

"Maybe, but I'm not going to complain."

They rode in silence for a few minutes, and Mal contemplated the giant weight on her chest that had not gone away when she let her secret out, but rather had shifted into a new kind of pain, the dull, heavy weight of the Carsons' disapproval. What did it matter? she thought. She would be leaving. She watched the country turn into small neighborhoods, then mix with a few businesses, until they were on the one street that comprised downtown Hollow Bend. Billie pulled up behind a small, freestanding brick building with animal drawings taped to the windows.

"Kids do those," Billie explained. "To say thanks to my dad for saving their pets. He was so tickled by the first one, he hung it in the window, and now it's sort of a tradition."

"How do you see out?"

"There are strategically placed gaps in the artwork. Anyway, then I don't have to deal with curtains. Mal, you don't know what a huge help this is," she said, leading Mal into the office through a side door. They walked past rows of cages, most of which were empty except for a few thankfully sleeping dogs, and a cat nursing tiny, tiny kittens. "I'll give you the grand tour later, but I want to show you the office first, get it over with. Then if you decide to run, I'll disarm you with kittens."

Mal laughed, then peeked around Billie's shoulder into the office.

It was a disaster. There were papers all over the floor—they really must have fallen on Billie's head. Drawers were open in the tall filing cabinets against the wall. Overflowing files were stacked haphazardly on a long, low cabinet under the window. There was a desk, sort of, and a computer, barely discernible under the envelopes and invoices and what looked like a library book called *Accounting for Dummies*. It was such a mess there was barely room to step into the office, and no clear way to start.

Mal was in heaven.

Chapter 16

Three days later Mal was still digging her way out of Dr. Monroe's paperwork, but she was starting to see the light at the end of the tunnel. She had set up a filing system that would manage the different bills and invoices, and downloaded long-overdue upgrades to their accounting software. She was putting the finishing touches on the vendor database when Billie poked her head in the office.

"Oh my gosh, we have furniture in here! Mal, this looks amazing."

"Thanks. Is it time to go? Hang on, I'm almost ready." Mal would stay there all night finishing if she could, but Billie had been faithful to her word and drove her home every night for supper. Not really home, though. Back to the Wild Rose.

She definitely would have stayed in town if she could. Libby was as kind as ever, and Mal could tell that she and Katie were trying to understand her situation, but there was still that tension, like they were dancing nervously around a river when they should just be getting into a boat and crossing it.

It didn't matter, Mal told herself. Luke would be back soon, and after she was done killing him, he would drive her back to DC, maybe hold her hand while she got a divorce, and she'd be done with the Carsons forever. They would just be a fond memory of some people who had once showed her kindness.

"I can't take you home tonight. Sorry, I forgot to tell you. I've got a date," she said with a sly smile.

"Oh!" said Mal, wondering how long it would take her to walk back to Wild Rose. If she left now, she could be there by dinner. Tomorrow. Still, she couldn't begrudge a small-town girl her love life. "That's great."

"I have to go home and change, obviously," Billie said, indicating the Big Bird scrubs she was wearing. "Trevor's not coming to get me until eight, but it's going to take me a while to start looking like a girl again."

"I'm sure you'll look gorgeous."

"Coming from you, that means a lot." When Mal looked confused, Billie continued. "Because you're gorgeous. You've got that city confidence."

Mal patted her fake blond hair knotted into a ponytail with a pencil. "Yes, it's very chic. This is what all the women are wearing at the country club."

"You know what I mean."

"Not really."

"Sure you do. You're wearing jeans and a T-shirt just like everybody else, but they're just a little different. More stylish."

"They're from Target."

"Listen, Mal," said Billie, laughing, "I'm not going to argue with you about how gorgeous you are! I have to get gorgeous myself. Keith will be here in a few minutes to pick you up."

Keith. Keith was like dancing around whitewater rapids, when all she really wanted to do was jump right in. They had been avoiding each other as much as Libby would allow. Mal wasn't even sure she had convinced him that she had kissed him first. She wasn't sure why it continued to matter.

"Listen, when he gets here, don't tell him I'm going out with Trevor. He gets all protective-older-brother and I don't need that right now. I just need to get laid, and I'm pretty sure Trevor puts out on the first date."

Mal laughed. "OK. I won't tell him. Be careful."

Keith was not, by nature, a curious person, but he hated secrets and he hated Mal's secret most of all. Married. Who was this guy she was married to? What the hell was wrong with him that he could just let her go? He wasn't sure he bought Katie's story about how this Michael was a jerk so Mal ran. If every woman who thought *he* was a jerk ran away, well, he'd have . . . just about as many women around him as he did now. Women who put up with him only because they were related.

Vanessa had put up with him. In his memories, she always had the patience of angels, she walked on clouds, she doled out kindness with a virtuous hand. The truth, he knew, had a few more shadows. She'd wanted Keith to take over Dr. Monroe's practice and grow it, but she'd hated that he worked so much. She'd hated living at Wild Rose, although she liked the little cottage well enough. She'd wanted to live in town, to raise their kids in a neighborhood with other kids and neighbors close enough to wave to.

She'd tried to get Katie to wear lip gloss.

Keith would give anything to have her back. Missing her was a constant dull ache in his heart, one that flared up unexpectedly, when he was working, when someone turned their head just so. He needed to move on, he knew he needed to let her go, but then the sun would slant through the trees and he would remember standing in the kitchen while she explained the difference between cooking oils and why it was important that the next time he go to the store for her, he get her the one she actually asked for. There were so many things he couldn't do without her. He couldn't cook. He couldn't laugh. He couldn't have kids.

What if their baby had been his only chance to have a family?

Bob nudged him in the shoulder, snapping Keith awake. He was running a few of the horses around in a pen, but Bob was in a mood, which meant she wasn't going to run unless someone sat on her back and made her.

"Are you really doing this today, Bob? I've got a lot of work to do." No, he didn't, but he didn't want to ride. When he rode, he had time and space to think about things and he had done enough thinking already.

Plus, he had to pay bills.

That was enough to send him to the barn for a saddle.

Maybe he should do what Libby said and ask Mal for help. Billie Monroe sure seemed happy with her work, and Mal would probably be happy to lend a hand—she seemed to have some sort of calculator for how much she owed them for . . . harboring her, or whatever they were doing.

Still, the less he interacted with her the better. He had managed to avoid speaking more than three words to her since she'd started with Dr. Monroe. It was rude, no doubt, but he couldn't handle more. When he talked to her, that dull ache lifted. She made him smile.

But she had lied to him—to all of them—about who she was, which was someone else's wife. Maybe not for much longer, but that didn't change the lie. He needed her to just go back to where she belonged so he could forget about her and go on with his pathetic life, pining for a family he would never have while not ever talking to anyone he wasn't related to. Then he would be happy again.

He shook his head as he pulled a saddle down off the rack. He was delusional, he knew that, but it was better to be delusional than to go crazy trying to reconcile warm feelings toward a woman who pretended to be his brother's fiancée but turned out to be someone else's wife. It was better to be delusional than to admit that, in these three days he had been avoiding her, he'd missed her smiling at him and laughing at him and the way she sort of scrunched up her mouth when she was concentrating on something. The way she jumped headlong into things she had no idea how to do. And those jeans. They weren't particularly tight or fashionable, but they sure fit.

Much better to be delusional.

He heard a high-pitched beeping coming from the tack room. He knew what it was. Mal had left her cell phone in a pocket of one of the barn coats, which he'd discovered the first time it went off at seven that morning. He had been ignoring it, but not ignoring it well enough to know that this was at least the tenth time it had rung, and he hadn't even been in the barn all day.

He pulled it out after it stopped ringing. Seventeen missed calls. He should put it back and walk away, he knew that. But he clicked on the button that showed him the numbers anyway. He scrolled down. Seventeen missed calls from the same number. He stared at the number for a bit; an East Coast area code that looked familiar from one of their tack suppliers, the expensive one that Katie used to buy fancy stuff for kids who were doing show jumping. He should maybe call Mal at Dr. Monroe's. Maybe it was an emergency. But he would be picking her up in a few hours, and he didn't like the idea of interrupting her bookkeeping high (surely, she had an illness) to have her call someplace she didn't want to be.

He was lost in his deliberation, and he nearly jumped out of his boots when the phone went off in his hand. Without thinking, he pressed the OK button and started to say, "Hello."

"Jesus Christ, finally. Mal, I have better things to do than wait around for you to pick up your phone. Do you know how many times I've called? I don't appreciate—"

"Mal's not here right now," Keith said, trying to relax his grip on the phone. It wouldn't do to break it, especially since it wasn't his. "Can I take a message for her?"

"Are you kidding me? Where the hell is she? What does she have to do that's so damned important she can't talk to her *husband*?"

Ex-husband. Almost. The guy she'd been running from. Keith switched the phone to his other ear and shook out his hand. Took a deep breath. "She's at work."

"Work? Are you kidding me? That woman hasn't worked a day in her life."

"Well, she's working now."

"Unbelievable. Do you know how many years I had to support her? Even when I was going through medical school, I had to carry her financially. Now she leaves and she suddenly develops a work ethic."

"That's not how I heard it."

"What?"

"I'll tell her you called."

"Wait, hold on a minute. Who the hell is this?"

"Keith."

"Well, who are you, Keith? Are you her new boyfriend?"

"No."

"What the hell are you doing answering her phone?"

"She left it behind."

"Of course she did. That girl can't do anything on her own. Did you know that I had to show her how to iron my shirts? It was like she'd never seen a can of spray starch."

Keith wasn't sure what spray starch had to do with a forgotten cell phone, so he didn't say anything.

"Listen, Keith, is it? I'm sorry you've been saddled with her for, what, it must be weeks now. I know she's high maintenance and she can't get anything done on her own. She's been a real drain on me. Did she tell you I'm a doctor?"

He seemed to want a response, so Keith said, "Yeah."

"Pediatric oncology. Heartbreaking stuff, but it's really important work. I'm saving lives, Keith, and it has been so hard for these last seven years to go to work all day, try to cure cancer—cancer, Keith—

and come home to find no food in the house, mess everywhere. She's a drain, Keith. She's sucking the life out of me. I'm still young, I still have a lot to offer a woman. But does she see it? No. She barely even speaks to me! I deserve more than that, don't you think?"

"I think you'll get whatever you deserve," Keith said.

"Exactly! And she leaves without any word about where she is. Where the hell are you, anyway?"

"Kentucky."

"Kentucky, Christ. What the hell is in Kentucky?"

People with manners, Keith thought.

"I still can't believe she just up and left. How selfish can you be? Didn't she think that people would be wondering where my *wife* is?"

Ex-wife. Almost. "Sounds like it might be a relief for you."

"Oh, don't get me wrong, Keith. It's opened my eyes to a lot, to how much better my life will be without her. I just don't appreciate having to go to hospital functions on my own and having to field questions about where that charming—ha—wife of mine is. Those looks of pity when I have to say 'trial separation.' But I have to tell you, aside from that, my life has been much easier, really eye-opening. That's why I've got these divorce papers here, just waiting for her to sign, and I can't wait around for her forever. I've got a life to lead, you know?"

"Sure."

"Write it down, please. Mallory is useless at remembering things. Write this: Dear Mallory, pull it together. You wanted this divorce and, for once, you got it right.

"Am I going too fast?"

"I'll tell her," Keith said. Before Michael could thank him kindly for relaying the message, he hung up.

Keith pulled into the parking lot behind Dr. Monroe's office promptly at five. It hadn't changed a bit, and apparently neither had he; on instinct, he pulled into the doctor's spot. He wasn't a doctor here anymore. He was starting to pull out to find a spot on the street when Billie came out of the office wearing some of the most ridiculous scrubs he had ever seen in his life. Was that Big Bird?

"Hey, you can't park there—oh, hi, Keith. I didn't recognize your truck."

He turned off the truck and got out. "I traded with my dad. Didn't need that big diesel anymore."

"No, I guess you wouldn't when you're not hauling medical equipment around."

They stood there, just looking at each other.

Billie sighed. "OK, I won't give you a hard time about coming back to work here if you don't give me a hard time about going out with Trevor tonight."

"Trevor! That guy—"

Billie held up her hand. "Deal?"

"Deal," Keith grumbled. Then he pulled Billie close and gave her a noogie.

"Hey! Quit it!"

"Are you okay? I heard—" Mal stopped abruptly when she saw Keith with Billie in a headlock. "Um, I heard shrieking."

"Yes," Billie said in a muffled voice from Keith's armpit. "Keith is just being a—" She pulled her elbow up, aiming for his groin. He saw her, though, and released her just in time. "Good reflexes, old man."

"Not too old to kick Trevor's—"

"Hey," Billie said, pointing her finger at Keith. "You promised."

"Fine. You ready?" he said, turning to Mal. He tried not to let the catch in his breath show. She was just wearing jeans and a T-shirt, and her hair was pulled back in that ridiculous messy way, with a pencil sticking out of it. How did she take his breath away?

"Sure," she said, giving him a funny look. "Actually, just give me a second to finish up in here."

"Are you really just finishing something up, or are you going to start something new that takes hours?" Billie asked.

Mal laughed. "No, I promise I'm just finishing. Five minutes," she said to Keith.

"I know how you get, that's all. This woman has a sickness," Billie said. "And I have a date," she said to Mal.

"OK! OK, just let me get to it." She walked back inside.

"Come on, you can wait for her inside." Billie said, holding the door for him.

"I'll just wait out here."

"Keith." She gave him a look, and just stood there, propping the door open with her hip, her arms crossed over her chest.

"Fine, I'll come in. But we have a deal."

Billie stuck her tongue out at him and followed him inside.

It was exactly how he remembered it, with pale blue walls and white tile and a general air of sterility. He started down that long hall that would lead to the waiting area, peeking into exam rooms, seeing a kid and his mom gently petting their dog as Dr. Monroe finished up a cast. He remembered doing that, and how Dr. Monroe had taught him that being a vet was about more than fixing the animal, that you had to take care of the human, too. Keith didn't know how many times he'd told worried kids to just be gentle with Fluffy or Mojo or Dino and make sure she took her medicine, how many times he'd told parents not to worry about the bill, Linda would work out a payment plan. For so many people, all that mattered was knowing their four-legged kid would be OK.

Having been on the receiving end of such sympathies, he didn't know how people could take it. Of course, things were probably different when you were talking about your wife rather than your dog. And she hadn't had a broken leg or a tapeworm.

There was no sense reliving the past, though. That was why he never came here; Dr. Monroe's practice was his past. His future was . . . Wild Rose, maybe, although lately his heart wasn't in it, not the way Katie's was. But it was his responsibility. Although suddenly the reasons *why* it was his responsibility were a little fuzzy. Why couldn't he move on with his life again? Why had he made this choice?

"There you are," said Mal, sticking her head out of the office door. "I'm almost done, I swear."

"Take your time." But hurry up.

He followed her into the office. That was the one place he didn't recognize. "They got office furniture?"

Mal laughed and leaned into the file cabinet, fishing. "That's what Billie said. I guess it's been buried."

"Mal, it looks great in here."

She pulled open another drawer. "Thanks. It took me a while to work out where things should go. I mean, I've done accounting before, but I've never worked with a vet or any doctor, so I had to really grill Billie on the workflow and . . ." She turned her head, still sandwiched between two file drawers. "Does this interest you at all?"

"It interests me that you're helping out a friend."

"Yeah, well," she said, and started to stand up.

"Whoa." And suddenly Keith was at her back, holding her head down into the file drawers.

"Hang on," he said, and pushed the top drawer closed. She just sat there, leaning over the bottom drawer, until she felt his hand on her back. "It's OK." He gently guided her up. "I didn't want you to hit your head."

"Wouldn't be the first time. Wouldn't be the first time today, actually . . ." She trailed off, looking around, placing a hand on his arm. He let her hold on until she was steady.

"Mal, come on!" Mal jumped a little at Billie's voice as it came barreling down the hall before her. "You promised . . . Hey, are you OK?"

"Yes, fine."

"Did you hit your head again? Girl, you've been working too hard. You need more fresh air. And I need to get—"

"Yes," Keith said quickly before she could finish the sentence. "We know."

Mal smiled, then turned to shut down the computer and gather her stuff.

"Is this it?" Keith asked, holding up her purse.

"Well, I was going to bring some of these," she pointed to a box of papers, the one messy spot in the office.

"No," said Billie, grabbing Mal's arm, then her purse. "We're leaving. It will all be here tomorrow."

The ride home was a little tense, but not as tense as, say, a war crimes trial. Despite his word, Keith had given Billie some, well, advice on how to handle Trevor, who was a troublemaker and who he thought was dating Katie. To which Billie responded that nobody goes out with Trevor for long. So Keith, like an idiot, asked what was the point, then, if you knew you were just going to get dumped? So Billie said that she wasn't going out with him because she wanted him to be her boyfriend. Then she said she wasn't going to talk to him anymore because he was getting that big-brother jaw clench and she didn't have time to argue with him *and* change out of her scrubs and into her date underwear. Then Mal piped in that he must really be worth it, and that it would take a lot to get her to wear uncomfortable underwear. At which Billie laughed and Keith practically ran to the car in an effort to stop picturing Mal in uncomfortable date underwear. He wasn't entirely sure what it was, but it sounded like something very . . . sexy.

"It's very sweet how protective you are of Billie," said Mal, who was fiddling with the radio.

"She doesn't like it."

"No, she doesn't. But you let her go anyway, so it's still sweet. Do you really only get country music down here?"

She flipped back and forth between the presets (all country, except for one for NPR, but even that was playing an old-timey bluegrass show). "Hey! This is that song we danced to! I can't believe I recognized it!" She turned to him, dancing in her seat. "I know a country song now."

He smiled at her as she continued to dance, then she slowed down as she listened to the words. "Save a horse, ride a cowboy," the singer sang out. She stopped. "Wow. Country music is dirty."

He laughed then. He shouldn't have laughed, because she looked over and caught his eye, and her gaze was so heated, so full, he swore he could see that her longing matched his, and that was no way to drive a car.

He cleared his throat and turned back to the road.

After a few minutes of silence—not at all awkward—Mal said, "Hey, do we have the same phone?" pointing to the center console.

"Oh, no, that's yours. You left it in the barn."

"Oh! No wonder it's been so quiet. Thanks for bringing it. I wonder if Luke called?" She started to scroll through the missed calls. He heard her sharp intake of breath, peeked over to see her looking pale and staring at the screen.

"You had a lot of calls today."

She didn't say anything, just kept scrolling down.

"Mal?" She wasn't really listening, so he figured now would be as good a time as any to confess. "I answered it."

"What?" she said sharply, turning to him.

"It kept ringing. I thought it might be an emergency. Or Luke."

"Was it?"

He sighed. "I talked to Michael."

She shrunk back in her seat. "Oh."

"I'm sorry, Mal."

"Sorry for picking up the phone or sorry for talking to my husband?"

"Ex, right?"

She turned away, blinking fast.

"You won't be married to him for much longer." He hoped. For purely platonic reasons, of course. No one deserved a toad like Michael.

She snorted. Then she sat back in her seat with a sigh. "I don't know if I can express how badly I want to be done with him, to have this divorce final and official so I can move on with my life. But the idea of facing him, even if I know it's for the last time . . . it still terrifies me. More than the idea of being on my own for the first time in my life, more than the fact that I will have nowhere to live, no job, probably no money if he has his way, which he will. Every time I see him, he makes me feel so . . . small. I was just starting to feel regular-sized again."

Don't go, Keith thought. *Or come back. Come back and stay here.* But that was ridiculous, so he kept quiet until they pulled into the driveway. Peanut ran out to meet the car, jumping up and licking Mal's window. She laughed, then wiped her eyes.

Keith thought about the conversation he'd had with Libby that morning at breakfast.

"You know," she'd said as Keith was remembering the way Mal's shirt came untucked from the back of her jeans when she leaned over, "I think you should take that girl for a ride." He spit out his mouthful of coffee. "I just mean," Libby continued, handing him a napkin, "that she said she's never been on a horse before, and here she is, cooped up until Lord knows whenever Luke moseys back here. Show her around, make her fall in love with the place. Then maybe she'd make that pretend engagement real."

Keith hated to think about Mal marrying his no-good brother, but he hated even more to think about her leaving. Keith rubbed his chin and reached for a biscuit. "I'll think about it." But he knew he would think of no such thing. The farther he stayed away from Mal, and her lips, the better.

"Hey," he said to Mal now before she could open the car door. "Let's go riding tomorrow."

"Horseback riding?" She looked surprised—not as surprised as he was, though. What was he thinking?

"Yeah. You said you've never been, and you're leaving soon, right?"

"As soon as Luke can take me."

"So let's do it. Tomorrow."

She smiled at him and this was why he should have stopped to think about taking her riding, because if he had known she would smile at him like that and if he had known what it would do to his heart, he never would have asked. It felt amazing, and it hurt a little, too. "Tomorrow," he said, then climbed out of the car to pull Peanut off the door so Mal could get out.

Chapter 17

Mal could feel Keith watching her and it was making her nervous. She was trying to decide if it was making her more nervous than being several feet off the ground on a creature that could kick her skull in when Keith said, "Relax, Mal. You're making him nervous." Which made her even more nervous. What happened when a horse got nervous? A horse named Bullet? Sure, Keith said the name was a joke, that he was old and slow, but still. Would Bullet bolt? Bolt, then bite, then . . . the alliteration of her paranoia made her giggle.

Nervously.

"Hey."

Keith had ridden up next to her and placed his hand over hers, which were squeezing the life out of the reins. Bullet turned his head and tried to bite Blue, the horse Keith was riding, which made Mal gasp and squeeze harder. She would never survive a horse fight.

"Mal."

She looked up from where Bullet and Blue were engaged in a fierce battle of wills (aka trying to ignore each other) and looked over at Keith. His cowboy hat sat low on his forehead, shielding his face from the late morning sun, but his eyes still found hers. He was so sure and confident on Blue. He squeezed her hands on the reins, and in his eyes she saw, "You can do this."

So she closed her eyes, took a deep breath and, with the reassuring pressure of Keith's big hands on hers, she relaxed.

Keith could feel it the minute Mal let go—the fear, the tension, whatever it was that had her sitting ramrod straight and pulling poor

Bullet to a stop while telling him to go. Of course, her eyes were closed, so he wasn't sure how to tell her to get moving.

"Ready?" he asked, leaning back into Blue's saddle.

"Not really," she replied, opening her eyes and looking ahead with determination. "But OK. Let's go."

She had grit, he thought suddenly. She was scared, but she would cowboy up.

She was made to be out here.

And he was mooning over a woman who was married. *Almost not married,* the voice in his head reminded him. But still, technically, married. But then she turned around to face him, her brown eyes strong and focused, not on her fear, but on the adventure. They were practically sparkling with it.

"I'm ready."

All told, she followed directions pretty well. Bullet responded to her tugs on the reins, although he was less inclined to speed up with her halfhearted kick to his sides.

"Mal, he's never going to go if you don't kick him a little harder." They had pulled up to a stop again while Bullet munched on some tall grass off the trail.

"I don't want to hurt him!"

"You won't hurt him. It's like using a firm voice to give a command. If you don't kick him harder, he won't know you're serious about wanting him to stop eating every five steps."

He thought he heard her mutter "command, confidence," and then Bullet was off. At a mildly fast walk, at least.

"It worked!" She turned around in her saddle and beamed at him. She looked so bright and surprised. She was glowing under the brim of the old cowboy hat she wore.

Dammit. Keith was a goner.

"Good work," he said, and pulled up to take the lead. Beyond the fields, they would pick up the old horse trail, then follow the creek up the hill a bit. It was a ride he had taken many times, usually to show the property off to prospective boarders.

He had no business being away from his work for several hours. Sure, the horses needed exercise, but there were more efficient ways to do that, ways that did not keep him out of his office when he had a pile of paperwork to deal with.

Then he heard her breathe, a deep, happy sigh that carried over the sound of clopping hooves. He looked ahead and smiled. The fields were laid out before them, and the hills were practically glowing in the distance, that mix of orange and yellow with a few spots of bright red. The colors rolled on, past the edge of his property line, past where they could see.

He had looked at those hills every day for his entire life and he always felt the same about them. He let out the breath he was holding, mirroring Mal's happy sigh.

Mal wasn't sure when she'd ever been so terrified and happy. She was not the sort of person who sought out adventure, and generally preferred her adrenaline levels normal and steady. Still, the quick ratcheting of her heart when Bullet finally decided to move—at her command—she could see why people were drawn to horseback riding. As she rode behind Keith, her focus shifting between the ground (far away) and Keith's strong back (also far—knock it off, Mal), she could feel herself learning Bullet's movements. When she sensed him wanting to linger over a tuft of grass, she swept her legs along his sides. When he nickered and let his gaze follow a bolting rabbit, she pulled the reins and set him back on course. As if he could sense when she most needed it, Keith would occasionally turn around and offer some terse advice or a nod of encouragement. Probably he was just checking to make sure she hadn't fallen off. As the morning rolled slowly into afternoon, she felt less nervous on Bullet and more in control.

It was not a feeling she was used to.

Eventually, Keith led them off the well-worn trail and they began to follow a stream. It was clear and wide in places, and Mal looked longingly at the grassy patches that blended into the creek bed. Riding was exhilarating, but her butt was getting sore.

So when Keith jumped off Blue and parked her in a small patch of grass, Mal was almost too grateful to be concerned about getting off the horse. Almost.

"I figure we can have lunch here," he said as she gripped the reins and looked over Bullet's side.

"You getting down?"

"Yes. Sure. Lunch."

"Do you need a hand, Mal?"

She looked over, expecting Keith to be laughing at her. She was probably five feet off the ground and she couldn't figure out how to get down. But he just reached one hand over Bullet's neck to steady him and put the other hand on the back of her saddle.

"Just take your right foot out of the stirrup. Good. Now lean over to me and swing that leg around."

As she did, Bullet moved a little and Keith grabbed her by the waist, saying "whoa" softly, and hopefully to the horse, and lowered Mal to the ground. He didn't move his hands right away. Mal didn't really mind.

Bullet and Blue were chomping happily in a small clearing as Mal spread out the blanket on the grassy bank. Keith unhooked the basket from Blue's saddle and looked hungrily at what Libby had packed. Some cold fried chicken, her famous potato salad, more oatmeal cookies than they could decently eat, and something wrapped in foil in a side pocket—candy? Libby was not a candy person. No.

Holy—

Libby had packed them condoms.

Where the hell was Miss Libby buying condoms?

"Anything good in there?" Mal asked as she kicked off her shoes.

"Uh." Keith shoved the condoms in his pocket and went over to join her on the blanket. It was one of the last warm days before winter started thinking about showing up, and Mal had set them up in a sunny spot. He pulled off his flannel shirt and let the warmth seep in through his T-shirt.

They ate, they made small talk. He found it easy to talk to Mal, and he didn't find it easy to talk to anyone. But as they passed the container of potato salad back and forth, he found himself not just answering her, but asking her questions. Where she grew up, what her folks were like, how she could possibly be almost thirty and never have been on a horse.

She laughed. He did love when she laughed.

"Have you ever been on a subway?"

He smiled over at her. "I took a bus in Lexington once."

"Hmm. Not the same thing."

"I've never even been on a plane."

"What? Not even on your honeymoon?"

He stilled.

"Sorry," Mal said quickly. "I didn't mean to—"

"No, it's OK. We didn't fly. We drove. To the Greenbrier in West Virginia."

"You honeymooned in West Virginia?"

"It's nice there. Too nice, really. We lasted one night, and then we rented a cabin in the state park."

"That sounds really nice, actually. Very romantic."

"That was sort of the idea."

A moment passed. Keith reached for a piece of chicken. "So where was your honeymoon?" he asked.

"The Bahamas. We took a plane."

He smiled. "Sounds nice."

"Yeah, it was nice."

"Hmm."

"Oh, no. It was nice. It was a beautiful resort, white sand beaches, amazing food. I think I gained five pounds."

"But?"

Mal picked at her cookie. "Well, I'm not much of a beach person. I mean, it was gorgeous and luxurious, like out of a magazine. But there was nothing to do, you know?"

"You couldn't find something to do on your honeymoon?"

She threw a crumb at him.

"It was just, I don't know. It didn't feel right." She took a bite of her cookie. "I guess I'm just not cut out for marriage."

Keith knew he shouldn't be asking the woman who was masquerading as his brother's fiancée when she was already married to another man any more about her views on marriage. "Why not?"

She snorted. "I'm just not that good at doing what someone else wants, I guess. I have to be free!" She flung her arms out, knocking her hat back.

"Marriage isn't about one person being in charge."

"No? You weren't the breadwinner? The man of the house?"

"No. I mean, yes, I was the man, but it was more like a partnership. Vanessa was good at some things, I was good at other things, and we made a life. Trust me, I was not in charge."

He looked over to see her looking at him funny.

"What?"

"Keith Carson, I do believe you are a romantic."

It was the last thing he expected anyone to say about him—ever—
and he barked out a laugh and rolled onto his back.

Mal leaned over him. "You laugh, but it's true. I can see it. You
pretend to be all gruff and serious, but you're secretly polite and
kind. You pretend to be all hard and business, but inside you're just
a softy."

He knew what she was saying was true, but he didn't want to hear
it, not from her. He didn't want to know how well she knew him.

So he did what he thought was the most expedient way of quiet-
ing her. He reached behind her neck, pulled her toward him, and
kissed her.

Mal could feel the instant Keith started thinking. His lips, at first
warm and soft, froze, and the hand at the back of her neck relaxed
its gentle pressure.

She liked that pressure.

She liked those lips. And, dammit, she liked Keith. Whatever
battle he was fighting with his conscience, she wanted to end it,
preferably with his lips going back to warm and soft.

She raised her head a little and opened her eyes.

"I'm so—"

"Don't you dare apologize."

Keith looked stunned.

"If you're really sorry for kissing me"—Mal punctuated her anger
with a poke to his chest—"then just shut up about it. A woman
doesn't like to hear a man's regrets."

"I don't—"

"But I'm not sorry. I wasn't sorry the other night and I'm not
sorry now. I like you, Keith. I like how you make me feel. I like that
you try to act like a jerk but you're hopeless at it. I like your hat and
I like how you fill your jeans."

Keith raised his eyebrow. Mal ignored him and soldiered on.

"I know being here is not right and that this fairy tale Luke
dropped me into is not going to last."

"You think mucking stalls is a fairy tale?"

"I do. I mean, not all of it. The details are not important, Keith.
I'm talking about this place. I've never seen any place so beautiful."
She swept her arm around her. "And Libby's cooking and the

horses and the way all the men are so handsome. It's like this place is enchanted. And I know I have to leave soon, to go back or go . . . somewhere, I don't know. But I'm here now and I like the way you kiss, so please, please don't apologize out of politeness to me because I'm. Not. Sorry."

Mal was a little breathless and as he continued to stare up at her, she could feel a blush work its way up her neck and into her cheeks.

He was just staring. She couldn't stand it.

So she braced her hands on his chest, leaned down, and kissed him.

Keith was through with thinking. He knew that Mal's speech gave him permission to do what, he had to admit, he had been thinking about since he first saw her on Luke's arm. Such a short time and already she had invaded every part of his life.

But thinking prevented him from feeling her kiss, the pressure of her small hands on him, the rise and fall of her chest against his.

He brought his hand up from her neck to the back of her head, twining his fingers through her hair and pulling her even closer. She made a sound—Surprise? Pleasure?—and he deepened the kiss, welcoming her curious tongue and making his own sounds as she shifted to a better angle.

He liked her where she was, sprawled on top of him, so he moved his hand to her waist to keep her there. But then that wasn't enough, so he slid his hands down, over her bottom to the back of her knee, which he hitched up to his hip, opening her on his lap.

She raised her head with a little gasp of surprise, then one corner of her mouth lifted in a smile.

Keith couldn't have formed a rational thought if the house was on fire. That little smile from her, and his heart told him, yes, finally, take what she's giving.

Growling, he rolled her over and pinned her underneath him. Her lips found his again and he felt her arms go around his broad shoulders. He kissed her, her lips, her cheek, her jaw. When he kissed the pulse at her neck, she let out a little gasp. He smiled into her skin, so soft, and licked her there.

Chapter 18

It was just her neck, no big deal. So why was she writhing under him like a snake? As Keith shifted his lips from one side of her neck to the other, she ran her hands over his shoulders and back. She loved the solid feel of him, the way his shoulders worked with the effort of holding himself up. But she wanted him closer. She sought his mouth again. Closer. She wriggled one of her legs from under his and brought it up to his hip. Closer. The word pounded an insistent rhythm in her brain as she shifted her hips beneath him, feeling his hardness against her. Closer, dammit. Closer. She ran her hands down his sides—he was so solid—and over the back of his jeans, then up to his waist, where she maneuvered a hand under his T-shirt. The skin of his back was hot; he had the same fever she did. She ran her hands up his back, feeling each muscle twitch under her fingers.

He sat up abruptly and she started to protest—don't you dare apologize now—but he looked at her, his green eyes dark with hunger, and tore the shirt over his head. She immediately reached for him, running her fingers over the dark hair on his chest, loving the sensation of rough hair over solid muscle. And he was solid. Her hand spanned across one pectoral in awe. Thank God for farm muscles. She ran her hands over his chest, over the roundness of his shoulders, drawing a line with her finger where his tan started. She'd had no idea a farmer's tan could be so sexy.

But then she was distracted by the feel of Keith's fingertips on her chest, slowly working the buttons on her shirt, gently brushing the skin between her breasts. He breathed out a word that sounded like "beautiful" and kissed her there, his tongue following his fingers as he pulled open her shirt, baring her bra to the sunshine. He ran his hands gently over the silk and lace, then moved his hands around to unclasp her bra in the back. It didn't work one-handed, so he used both. Mal sat up a little to give him more room. He wasn't getting it. And he was starting to curse, and Mal didn't want to risk losing the mood, so she slapped his hand away, unhooked her bra, and threw it across the blanket. They sat there for a second, half naked in the sunshine, and then he was on her again, pulling her close, gasping at the sensation of skin on skin.

Closer, she thought again, and reached down for the clasp of his jeans. He did the same for her, and soon they both had their jeans around their ankles, too foggy with lust to figure out how to get them over their shoes. Mal just gripped Keith's shoulders tighter, held him closer. He pulled back for a second and reached into his pocket. In no time, the condom was on and Mal pulled him back to her, lifting up one knee to let him in. It was awkward, their legs tangled in their bunched-up jeans, but not so awkward that Keith couldn't find his way to the center of her, taking it slow and easy until she was full, and then, as her nails started to dig into his back, faster, harder, higher. She cried out his name as she went up and over, shaking, gripping his back. He dug his fingers into her hips, buried his face in her hair, and followed right after her.

What the hell had he just done?

Had *they* done, really?

Mal shivered in his arms. He ran his hands through her hair, down her back. He wasn't sure if she was cold or crying or what. He couldn't tell anything with her head buried in the crook of his neck. She felt good there, like she fit, but he didn't want to get too comfortable because what if she was upset? He thought probably she had enjoyed it as much as he had—enjoyed was an understatement—but now that he couldn't see her face, he didn't know. Did she regret it? Already? Jesus, what kind of animal was he—he found out she wasn't engaged to his brother and he waited, what, three days before he jumped on her? Yes, of course, he wanted her—from the moment he saw her he'd wanted her—but come on. He wouldn't blame her if she hated him.

"Keith." Her voice was muffled against his chest.

"Hmm?"

"You're squishing me."

"Oh!" He jerked his hands off her hips like she was on fire. Jesus, he was probably bruising her.

"Don't let go of me," she said, placing a hand on his neck. OK. He could do that. He could hold her.

"You're freezing," he said, running his hands up and down her shivering back.

"I'm naked and there's a breeze."

He scooted them to the edge of the blanket and pulled the other end over them. His butt was still hanging out, but he wasn't the one who was cold.

"Hmm." She sighed and snuggled into him, pulling the blanket tight across his back. He felt her relax and his heartbeat slowed to match hers. He closed his eyes.

"I don't know if I can get back up there," Mal said as she gripped the sides of Bullet's saddle.

"You did a lot of riding today."

Mal blushed.

But she laughed when she turned to see Keith's neck turning red, too.

She mounted, with Keith's blushing help, and they rode back. Keith was downright talkative—for Keith, anyway. Great outdoor sex really seemed to open him up. He pointed out spots where he and Luke used to play cowboys, where Katie snuck up on Luke and one of his girlfriends and put a frog in her purse.

"We heard her scream clear across to the barn."

Mal laughed. "I bet Luke was pretty mad."

"At first, but I think he got a lot of mileage out of comforting the girlfriend."

Mal thought for a second, thinking of the most delicate way to say this. "So, how much of a slut is Luke?"

Keith looked back at her with a smile. "He's a guy, he's not a slut."

"From what I've heard, he's had a new girlfriend every week since he was twelve. He's sort of a slut."

"Maybe. He's just . . . unsettled."

"Unsettled? Like crazy?"

"No, that's not what I mean. He's not like me and Katie. We're homebodies, me more than Katie. Even going to vet school in Lexington was tough for me."

"You didn't like school?"

"I didn't like the city. Too many people, too much traffic."

Mal had been to Lexington. She was definitely never taking Keith to DC.

Not that she was taking him anywhere.

"So you left the big city to come back to the farm?"

"Well, back to Wild Rose, but my plan was to take over Dr. Monroe's practice. Then . . ."

"Then?" Mal knew what came next, but her poor jealous heart needed to hear him say it.

"Then Vanessa died, and our baby. And I've just been . . ."

"Managing?"

"Yeah."

She wanted to know what he planned to do now, if he would stay at Wild Rose forever. But he muttered, "It's been three damn years," and she was afraid to ask him about the future.

"There's so much of her here. It's hard for me to forget."

"Is that what you want? To forget?"

"No! No, of course not. I just wish there was a way for me to . . ."

"Move on?"

"No. That means forgetting her."

"Do you really think you'll ever forget her?"

"I don't know. I just know it's been three damn years and sometimes it still feels like it was yesterday."

Mal didn't say anything. What could she say? She was grateful for the horse distance between them. It helped her curb the impulse to reach for his hand, or to touch his cheek.

"Sorry. This is weird for me to talk about, considering."

Considering they just had sex on a blanket.

Great, Mal thought. *Now here comes the regret.*

"I guess being close to someone again just brought it up. I haven't, you know, since . . ."

"Really? Three years? Wow."

He looked back with a crooked smile. "I'm feeling insulted here."

"Actually, I'm a little flattered."

"You should be. I mean——" Keith flushed. "I mean I wanted to do that. With you."

Mal smiled. "Good. Me, too."

They were back at the barn. Keith dismounted and helped her down.

"So, do you want to do it again?"

"Now?"

"No! I mean, not that I don't want to, but, um, I mean go out some time. After you get divorced. Since you're not engaged to my brother and all."

Chapter 19

One week later, Mal stood in front of the bathroom mirror, toothbrush poised, and contemplated her face. It was the same face she'd always seen, sort of average-looking. A guy she went out with when she was a freshman told her it was appealing because it was so symmetrical. Not beautiful, but appealingly symmetrical. That's what she got for thinking an art student would be romantic. That was a long time ago. Not long before she met Michael, though, which made it feel like even longer. She had the feeling that she was looking at herself from a distance, her foggy reflection just starting to come in clearer. Maybe she needed glasses.

The badness of her hair was taking on a certain urgency. Katie's friend, Jack, was coming over this afternoon to check on the horse he was boarding at the Wild Rose. It had been a long time since Mal had seen anyone from the outside world, it seemed. In the week since she and Keith had made love (she still blushed at the thought), her time had been taken up with working at Dr. Monroe's, coming home and helping Libby, and trying to help the Carsons around the farm, then dropping into bed exhausted. The time or two Katie had gone out with friends, Mal was too tired to join them. She hadn't even had time to go out on that date with Keith. It seemed that whenever she was free, he was meeting with suppliers or had an urgent farm job to take care of.

Beyond just seeing an outsider for the first time, she was also a little wary of Jack—he was a hairdresser in Lexington.

It had been a few months since her last trip to the salon; once Michael wasn't insisting on it—or paying—she didn't see the point. She had changed so much since she'd arrived at Wild Rose. She could handle a wheelbarrow. She used her first paycheck to buy a pair of work boots. The urgency she had been feeling to go back to her old house and get her old clothes—she was starting to see different options. Wheelbarrows and work boots. Huh. Anyway, blond hair made her look washed out, made her brown eyes dim. Of course, the massive roots she was currently sporting weren't helping at all. Not that Keith seemed to mind. He found her plenty attractive.

She blushed, remembering the strong hold he'd had on her head as he kissed her. It was a strange thing, watching in the mirror as the blush crept up her neck and into her cheeks. She was not a very cute blusher, she thought. She looked sort of like she had a disease. But, well, she was willing to put up with that if it meant . . .

If it meant what? Was she really going to participate in any more blush-worthy activities with Keith? He made her feel . . . amazing. He felt amazing. He was warm and giving and completely transformed by their intimacy. How did he see her? Dark roots and disease-blushed? Had he told her she was beautiful? This man of few words, how had he made her feel beautiful?

What the hell was she thinking? What did it matter? She was here temporarily. Just until she figured out what to do next. Just to get some space from Michael, get her head on straight, get divorced, and move on. She could do anything she wanted, go anywhere. What was she going to do, live on someone else's horse farm and be a bookkeeper, sneaking around with a man who made her feel beautiful? She had never in her adult life been independent. She had never had her own apartment, one all to herself. She had never been alone, no matter how lonely she felt in her marriage. She could go to Arizona, or Milwaukee or Kansas. Or Italy. She'd never been to Italy. She could sip vino and eat pasta until her pants didn't fit, and work as a bookkeeper at some little tourist shop on the Mediterranean.

Mal snorted. Even in her wildest fantasies, the best career she could come up with was bookkeeper. Well, so what? It made her happy; she could make a living at it. She was already doing that in just a few weeks at Dr. Monroe's. She could stay here and get an apartment in town—if Hollow Bend even had apartments—and work for Dr. Monroe and . . .

No. If she stayed, she would want Keith, and he had too much baggage. She had too much baggage. Once was enough. She wouldn't fight for a man's affection again, because it was a fight she knew from experience she would not win. Bad enough to lose to a suburban bimbo; there was no way she could compete with a ghost.

Her phone rang, nearly vibrating off the bathroom counter. She grabbed it without thinking—Luke had said he would call her back today—and answered with her mouthful of toothpaste.

"Mallory?"

She spit into the sink. "Hi, Michael."

"Let me guess, you're still in Kentucky."

"Yes. I'm going to find out today when my ride back to DC will be available." Luke better have a frigging amazing excuse for making her wait.

"Well, listen, this weekend might not be a great time."

She froze. "What?"

Michael sighed. "I didn't want to have to tell you this until after you signed the papers, but it's taking so long that I just can't wait."

"What is it, Michael?"

"The truth is, Mallory, I've met someone else."

Relief floated out of her chest like a thousand butterflies. Very frigging poetic. "Bunny?" she asked tentatively.

Michael coughed. "I know what you're thinking, how could I betray you like this with your best friend?" Mal didn't quite remember Bunny being her best friend, but she kept quiet as Michael continued. "It just sort of happened. She was such a rock for me when you were freezing me out." Freezing him out after she asked for a trial separation but he still wanted her to cook him dinner. Freezing him out after she caught him in bed with a nurse, then Bunny, then another nurse. Then two nurses.

But Michael was pretty good at justifying his philandering—Mal was frigid, Mal was fat. The only thing new was Michael actually admitting that he and Bunny had a thing. He continued, "Eventually, well, I started to see all the things I loved about her. She's gorgeous, she takes care of herself—"

"I'm very happy for you, Michael. You two deserve each other."

"After what I went through with you, I'm glad you recognize that. Bunny would never play games with me the way you did."

"When did Bunny divorce Dr. Ashton-Pierce?"

Michael sighed. "They're still working on it. Dr. Ashton-Pierce is not giving up on her that easily, not that I blame him."

Mal knew she shouldn't ask, but she couldn't help it. "Is this going to cause trouble for you, though? What about the hospital?"

"I can take care of myself, Mallory."

"But Dr. Ashton-Pierce is your boss——"

"Yes, I'm well aware that he is above me, but frankly, he's an incompetent doctor. He's getting old. If the hospital isn't careful, he's going to make a major mistake and they're going to have a lawsuit on their hands. Bunny and I are getting out while we still have a chance to make something more of our lives."

"Michael, that sounds risky——"

"That's how it always is with you, isn't it! I take one step forward with my life, and you want to pull me back down to your pathetic level!"

"Michael, I——"

"Well, guess what, Mallory, I don't need you anymore. I never needed you! Bunny has shown me what a *real* wife can be like. I don't have to tell her that she needs to lose weight or dress better. She's *perfect*. She *gets it*. She gets *me*."

"Michael——"

"Don't talk back to me! You never respected me! Well, listen to me, Mallory. I've got these divorce papers here, and when I'm ready, you're going to sign them, not before, not after. And if you can't get that redneck boyfriend of yours to deliver you to me, I swear I will track you down and make you sign. When *I'm* ready. Do you hear me? Do you?"

"Yes, Michael."

"Good, I——"

Mal hung up. She looked in the mirror, her hand shaking, her knuckles white on the phone. He was moving on. She was glad. They would get divorced. She would have Luke drive her back to DC and make Michael give her the papers.

But she knew Michael. She knew he would find a way to keep her tied to him forever. A panic welled up in her chest and she couldn't breathe. She would never be rid of him, no matter how far she went. He would keep this tie to her always. He would never divorce her——what was the point in trying? She looked down at the phone in her hand. It was ringing again; he was calling her back.

"No!" she shouted, and threw the phone against the bathroom wall, where it shattered.

She turned back to the mirror, eyes wild and red, hair sticking out, with a stupid fake blond dye job that he had insisted on, so she could match the other wives. She looked nothing like them. She looked like a ridiculous brunette with a lousy dye job.

"That's it." She sniffled, straightening her shoulders. "No more." She dug around in the drawer until she found a pair of scissors. She had at least an inch of hair to work with. Just an inch of her natural hair color. She barely knew what that was anymore. Brown, obviously. Boring, plain. But it was hers, dammit. It was *her*.

When Katie found Mal an hour later, she was still standing in front of the mirror, scissors in hand, surrounded by piles of blond hair. Most of the blond was gone from her head, but there were still several ragged inches on the ends.

"Holy crap, Mal," Katie whispered. "What the hell did you do?"

"I was trying to give myself a bob. I'm hoping if I stare at it long enough, it will start to look good."

"It's not . . . bad, precisely. A little, um, patchy."

"I was trying to make it even. Maybe if I——" She reached up for a longer piece behind her ear.

"No!" Katie grabbed the scissors. "No. Don't . . . don't cut any more, OK?"

Mal dropped her head into her hands. "I was just trying to get rid of the blond."

"OK. Uh, oh, God, Mal, don't cry, please." Mal's shoulders shook. "Mal, it's not that bad. It's kind of, you know, punk." Mal's shaking moved to her whole body, and she had to sit on the bathroom floor. When she moved her hands away, there were tears streaming down her face. And, Katie was relieved to see, a huge smile.

"I've never cut my own hair before," Mal said when she got her breath back.

"Really? I never would have guessed."

"It's really terrible, isn't it?"

"I am definitely the wrong person to ask about style advice. But I don't know, it is a little funky. It could suit you." Katie pulled out her cell phone. "It just needs a little help."

* * *

An hour after that, Mal was surrounded by even more hair. And a small-framed man in a cowboy hat.

Katie's best friend, Jack, stood behind her, wielding his hairdresser's scissors uncertainly.

"Are you sure? That's awfully short. Not that you don't have the face to pull it off, honey," he added quickly.

"I don't care what it looks like, I'm just sick of being a blonde."

"I know we just met, but so am I."

"Exactly. So if you just chop it all off, my natural snooze brown will grow back."

"I did bring my kit," he said, indicating a large red toolbox in the doorway of the bathroom. The top was flipped open to reveal more scissors, combs, and strange tubes of things Mal was, unfortunately, very familiar with.

"Can't you just cut it? See what it looks like?"

"Well, since those Carson boys are taking such good care of my horse, I might as well give the lady what she wants."

As Jack chopped the remaining ends of her fried blond hair off, Mal closed her eyes. The gentle *pft, pft, pft* of the scissors near her scalp was oddly relaxing. Jack kept up a quiet hairdresser's banter with her as he tugged and snipped: Where are you from? How long have you been here? Your husband did what? Mal wanted to sit there forever. Finally, she understood why women went to the salon so often—the quiet conversation, the peaceful attention of having a man touch your neck, turn your head, assess your face like it was a masterpiece.

"I don't think we'll color it. You have some subtle red tones I could play up, but let's get you used to the cut first. Besides, I don't want to get color on Miss Libby's floor or I'll be down there all day scrubbing it out. And I can think of much better things to do on my knees in this house."

Mal kept her eyes closed, but raised an eyebrow.

"Those Carson boys, mmm," Jack said as he started to section her hair. "I had my hopes up for Luke—he's so easygoing and I thought I saw him looking my way a few times. Turns out his gaydar is way off and he thought I was making a move on his sister. Still, that protective-mother-bear routine—" Jack shivered.

"He does have a protective streak."

"Speaking of bears, Keith is the one you want to watch out for. I don't usually like my men hairy, but I would be willing to make an exception for that one."

Mal blushed, remembering how Keith's hands heated her skin, how his hairy chest felt against her naked breasts.

"Oh, I see what's going on. Someone has a preference for the elder Carson."

"No, it's nothing, it's—"

"Um, sister in the room!" Katie held her hands over her ears.

"It's nothing. I'm sure it's nothing."

"Mal, everyone knows you're bonking my brother."

"What do you mean everybody knows?"

"The two of you are wandering around grinning like lunatics, and suddenly you're not making any mistakes with the chores. I mean, you're learning," she added quickly, when Mal started to protest. "But there's no way I could get away with half of the shit you do. Just don't make me slap you for breaking his heart."

"I don't think he's in any danger. We're just . . ."

"Just sex?" Jack asked. "Spill it."

"Sister in the room!" Katie yelled.

"It's not. I mean, it is, but it's not. He hardly speaks, you know? But he makes me feel, I don't know, warm I guess. Safe and protected—which is how I feel with Luke—but warm. And beautiful."

They lapsed into silence, Mal thinking of the ways Keith could break her heart, Katie really hoping she would not have to hurt this nice woman, and Jack admiring his genius.

"OK, take a look." He nudged her shoulder and she opened her eyes.

The blond was definitely gone. Her hair was short—shorter than Keith's even. But it looked . . . good.

"I decided to give you the whimsical pixie cut. You've got the cheekbones for it. And it brings out those brown eyes. You'll knock 'em dead."

"Wow." She ran her hand up the back of her neck, amazed at how light she felt. "Is it going to look like this in the morning?"

"No, darling, you are going to have serious bed head. But take this"—he handed her a can of mousse—"and just run a little through your hair, and you should be good. Minimal fuss."

"Jack, she looks great! Mal, wow. That really suits you."

"Thanks, Katie. It looks really . . . me."

"Well, I am a miracle worker. Helps if you have a gorgeous canvas to work on, though." Jack winked at her. "And now, ladies, your hero must go." He quickly packed up his supplies and was out the door, leaving Mal and Katie to scramble behind him.

"What? Aren't you going to stay for dinner? Libby will want to visit."

"As much as I would love me some of Libby's home-cooked deliciousness, my figure would not," he said, pinching his waist. "Anyway, I have a date."

"Who with? In town?"

"Someone who's none of your business."

"Why does a gay man in a tiny redneck town get more dates than I do?" Katie asked as he left.

"Because I'm not blind to what's in front of me," Jack shouted over his shoulder as he headed down the stairs.

"What's he yelling about?" Chase asked, coming in to wash up for dinner.

Katie looked at him, then turned away. "Don't you ever eat dinner at your own place?"

"Not when the company is so good here," he said, pulling her ponytail. She slapped his hand away, then chased him through the house. They almost ran over Keith, who was coming in from the barn. Peanut, who only followed him when Mal wasn't nearby, tore after them. Libby hollered for Keith to control his dog, for Katie and Chase to stop acting like children and wash up for dinner, and for Cal to come to the table.

"Where's Mal?" she asked Keith, as if he would know.

"Here," came a voice from the stairwell. Keith watched as she came down the stairs slowly, worrying her bottom lip. He stood there with his mouth open in surprise.

"Whoa," he said on an out breath, then moved to greet her at the bottom of the steps. He ran his hand over the short hairs at the nape of her neck as if savoring the smooth yet sharp texture. He looked into her eyes, "Mal," he whispered, cupping her face, rubbing his thumb gently over her cheek.

Mal knew that look of Keith's already—he was going to kiss her. But his entire family was standing in the doorway to the kitchen, gawking. They seemed to fade as his face moved closer to hers. "You like it?"

"You look—"

She never did get to find out what he was going to say—Beautiful? Amazing? Delicious?—because he was barreled into her by a force from behind. Why were people always getting knocked over in this house? It was like a Benny Hill movie. It was, as usual, Peanut, who had clearly been apart from his new favorite human for too long. Since three legs made stairs a little difficult for him, Mal broke from Keith (the smart thing to do, surely), and bent down to love on her dog.

Her dog. Hmm.

Peanut gave her that little curious sideways dog look—she did look pretty different, after all—but apparently she still smelled like Mal, because Peanut was all up in her face, licking her. Mal laughed.

"Well, now you'll have to wash your hands again before dinner," Miss Libby said, coming up and putting an affectionate hand on Keith's back. "Keith, sweetheart, take that mangy mutt out of here, and Mal, darling, you look gorgeous. A whole new woman."

Mal fingered her hair self-consciously. "Thanks. I feel like one."

Chapter 20

Mal couldn't sleep. She kept running her hands through what was left of her hair, loving how light it felt, remembering how Keith had fingered the short ends and looked at her with—what, admiration? Desire? Definitely desire. But then he had barely looked at her all through dinner, and ran off afterward, mumbling something about work to get done. She had been hoping to talk to him about taking a look at the farm's books; surely she had proven herself at Dr. Monroe's office. And he seemed to hate paperwork so much. Mal was sure she could help, at least to set up a filing system he could live with. Although Mal admitted a little selfish motivation—she had poked her head in the office once or twice over the past weeks, and the place was a mess. She could definitely get her hands dirty in there.

There were other selfish motivations, too. Like what Keith could do with his hands while she was filing.

Well, maybe after she was done filing.

One week. It had been one week since their horseback ride, and she was still blushing when she thought about it. Sighing, she resolved to stop thinking about it. Obviously they had both been caught up in a moment. It couldn't mean anything. She was still married to Michael, although it was just a legality that did not seem to stop Michael from moving on. So why shouldn't she? Because she hadn't met anyone she wanted to move on with.

Until Keith. Mal wasn't such a fool to deny the powerful attraction between them, the one that had snuck up so quietly she barely noticed it. Just like Keith, quiet and powerful.

But she was starting to think it was one-sided. If his recent absences meant anything, he was probably stewing in his brooding, silent way about how to get away from the nuisance Luke had dropped in their laps.

Oh, don't think about laps, Mal thought.

Mal was just finishing counting the cracks in the ceiling for the third time (still forty-three!) when she heard a tapping at the window. She froze up—she was on the second floor; what could that be? She looked down at the foot of her bed, where Peanut barked softly in his sleep.

"What a guard dog," she said, throwing the covers off and swinging her legs over the side of the bed. She snuck to the window in the ridiculous exaggerated tiptoe of Pink Panther movies. She peeled the curtain back half an inch, trying to see what was hitting the window.

It was Keith, standing under her window, throwing pebbles at the glass. She jerked her head back. Her heartbeat was going crazy—what was he doing outside the window?

"Mal!" she heard him whisper. He threw another pebble at the window, although this one was bigger than the others—it must have been, because with a night-shattering crash, the rock went through the glass.

"Shit," she heard from below.

"Keith, what the hell are you doing?" Mal was still trying to whisper, even though the whole house was probably awake by now.

"Mal! Mal, are you OK?"

"Yes, I'm fine! Stop throwing rocks at me!"

He sheepishly rubbed the back of his neck.

"What the hell is going on out here?"

Cal had come around the house. Carrying his shotgun.

"Pop, it's me."

"Boy, what the hell are you doing?"

"Throwing rocks."

"Why are you doing a damn fool thing like that?"

"I'm trying to get Mal's attention."

"Whatever happened to a phone call? Better yet, can't you wait until the morning? Some of us are trying to sleep."

"Can't you talk to me from there?" Mal whispered from the window. If she got too close to him, she would forgive him for ignoring her, and she wasn't ready for that. If she got too close, she would forget all of the reasons she was supposed to stay away. Why was she supposed to stay away, anyway?

"Um, it's sort of private."

"Are you just trying to make a move on me?"

"Yes." She didn't answer. "Is that OK?"

Mal heard the screen door slam. Either Cal had gone back inside, or he was coming around the house to shoot them both.

"If you don't come down here, I'll come up there."

"No, no, Peanut is up here. I'll come down."

"Peanut is up there with you? Nice guard dog."

"Hey, it's your dog," she said, ducking back into the window.

"He doesn't act like my dog," she heard him mutter.

Mal smiled, then shooed Peanut out of the room and started gathering layers, steering clear of the broken glass. She threw on a sweatshirt as she tripped down the stairs, and on the way out, grabbed the first coat she could find. She didn't know what Keith was up to, but she couldn't resist the opportunity to find out. She didn't know what was going on between them; had she ever felt a pull this strong to a man? Definitely not to Michael. She shook that thought out of her head. She would deal with Michael tomorrow. Tonight she would face the man waiting for her in the darkness.

Mal looked wary when she came out of the house. No surprise, really, since he had been avoiding her since their ride in the woods. But Keith had wanted to be ready the next time he came to her. He wanted to be the man she deserved, not a hollow shell. He was working on renewing his vet certification, starting to talk to Dr. Monroe about getting his place back. He was looking at some land closer to town; a man needed his own land. He had been packing up his old house, the one he had shared with Vanessa, storing the memories away and getting rid of the physical things he was holding on to because he didn't want to let go. He would always love Vanessa. But Mal had showed him another possibility beyond his half-life; she'd shown him that there was room in his heart for both of them, for the memory of Vanessa and for new experiences, to learn and grow with Mal.

It scared the hell out of him, and it scared him to keep it to himself. But he couldn't share all that with Mal yet, not when her future was so uncertain, and especially not when he hadn't said two words to her since they'd made love in the woods. But he knew she was worth the risk, worth working for, and if she was ready to be with him, he could show her that he had been ready all along.

Mal came toward him wearing what looked like every article of clothing she owned, with his dad's old coat over all of it. He could see her breath in the cold night air. She looked a little mad, but mostly curious. She looked adorable.

He was awkward and silent and probably creepy, just looking at her. Then she sighed and held out her hand. And that was that. He kissed her, and in that kiss, he felt all the love there was between them. He held her waist as she clung to his neck, but she kept slipping, so he moved his arms under her butt and hoisted her up so her mouth was flush with his.

He felt her shiver. "We should go inside," he said, a little breathless.

"Sorry, oh, God, I'm so heavy. Put me down, we'll go inside."

He kissed her quiet. "You're not too heavy." When she started to protest, he kissed her again. "I'm strong, dammit." And to prove it, he hiked her up higher on his body and kissed her again.

"I think your father is still out here."

"With a shotgun."

"Should I be nervous?"

"Only if you intend to take advantage of me."

"Well, I was considering it."

"Good." He kissed her again, lowering her feet gently to the ground.

He wrapped his arm around her shoulders and led her around the backyard to his bunkhouse. He noticed she was limping.

"Sorry, did I step on your toes?"

"No, I twisted my ankle running out of the house like a crazy person."

"Let me go look at it."

"It's fine. Although we should do something about that window. I don't think your father realizes that you broke it."

"OK, I'm going to board up the window before my father comes after me with his shotgun. Then I'm going to carry you inside and I'm not letting you out until we both are too limp too move."

"Hmm."

"You shouldn't bite your lower lip like that," he said as he held the door open for her.

"I can't help it. Nervous habit."

"Do I make you nervous?"

"A little!"

"Because I'm so big and manly?"

"Yes, that's it."

She continued to worry that lip.

"Mal."

"I'm sorry! It's not even a conscious thing! I just get around you and I want to eat my own face!"

He raised his eyebrow.

"I mean, I don't know, you don't make me nervous usually, but in situations like this"—she indicated the bedroom—"the whole thing is a little, I don't know, intimidating, I guess."

"I intimidate you?"

"Not you, specifically. Just, you know. Performance. Naked performance."

She went back to the lip.

"Let me do that for you," he said, leaning close and kissing her, pulling her lower lip between his. "I know this isn't going to make you stop worrying, but I'm just going to say it. And I'll keep saying it until you believe it. You have nothing to worry about, performance-wise or naked-wise. You get exemplary marks on both counts."

"Are you grading me?"

"I'm going to spank you if you don't get on with it."

She looked a little shocked (*and,* he thought, *a little interested?*), so he chased her around the bed.

Mal screamed and ran around the bed. She definitely wanted to be caught, and good thing, since she ran herself into the corner. She was cornered between the bed and Keith—not a bad place to be, really. She put her hands out in front of her. "Wait! Stop! What are you going to do?"

"I don't know yet. What do you want me to do?"

Mal was already breathless and he hadn't even touched her yet. "Um—"

"Too long. Take off your shirt."

"What?"

"If you can't decide what you want to do, I'll decide for you. I want you to take off your shirt."

"Hmm. Bossy," she said, but she complied. She took off one shirt—leaving a tank top on.

"I'm just getting started," Keith said, noticing she wasn't wearing a bra. He could see her nipples getting hard under the white tank top she wore.

"Take off *your* shirt. Fair's fair."

He reached down and pulled the hem of his shirt over his head. *He* wasn't wearing a tank top. Mal stepped forward—she just couldn't seem to look at that chest without touching it.

"Wait," he said, stepping back. "Not yet. You still have too many clothes on. It's not even."

Mal looked at him assessingly. She stepped back and shucked her jeans. "Your turn."

Keith was surprised at that—very pleasantly so. He doubted his jeans would come off that easily. He bent down and took off his right sock.

"Hey! Cheating!" Mal had taken her socks off with her shoes. She was standing there in just her tank top and panties.

"OK, I'll give you one more." He pulled off his other sock.

She lowered her eyes to his jeans. "Too chicken to take them off?"

"Why would I be chicken?"

"I'm not sure. Afraid I won't like it?"

"Oh, I know you like it. I remember. I remember how wet you were when I was inside you last time."

Mal's eyes widened. She'd never heard Keith talk like that before; she didn't think he had it in him. She kind of liked it. She definitely liked it, if the current state of her panties was any indication.

"Well, it's not even. I'm standing here in my underwear and you're still decently covered in outerwear."

"Barely," he said, and her eyes went to the bulge in his pants. She licked her lips and she swore she saw it give a little jump. "Anyway, you've got a shirt on."

"Barely!" she said right back at him, crossing her arms over her chest. He thought he would do just about anything to get her to stop covering those pretty breasts of hers.

"Fine, I'll be a gentleman," he said, unbuttoning and unzipping his jeans.

"Not fast enough," she said, stepping forward and easing his jeans over his hips. If, while she was at his waist, she happened to also hook her fingers into his boxers and pull those down as well so he was standing stark naked in front of her, well, was that her fault? She was a cheater. She ran her hands up his sides, across his shoulders, coming to rest on his pecs, rubbing the rough hair there.

Keith grinned to let her know that she might be in a little bit of trouble. Well, she had cheated. She took a step back, then turned away, aiming to go over the bed to the other side.

But she only got one foot on the bed. She began to vault herself over, but Keith grabbed her around her waist.

"Where are you going?" He pulled her to him, and she felt every naked inch of him against her.

"Over there," she said breathlessly.

"What are you going to do over there?"

Her nipples turned into hard pebbles against his palms.

"I forget."

He kissed her neck, one hand holding her waist while the other moved down over her stomach. When he reached the hem of her tank top, he slid his hand under it, then up to cup her breast in his bare hand. He squeezed gently, pinching her nipple between his fingers. Mal moaned and arched into him, rubbing her backside against his erection.

"Mal."

He pulled her hard against him, ripping her shirt over her head. Both of his hands went to crush her breasts, to crush her to him. She leaned into him, lifting her arms up and around his neck. She pulled his head toward her mouth, stretching around for a kiss. Her neck was straining as she tried to get closer, molding herself to him, getting inside of him. She opened her mouth wider, pushed her tongue against his, into his mouth.

Mal was definitely taking control of their kiss and he loved that. He loved her smooth back against his chest so his hands had complete access to her gorgeous, full breasts

It wasn't enough. He needed to get closer, he needed to feel her get higher. He let her control the kiss, but his hands controlled her body. He let go of her breasts, despite her whimper of protest. His hands snaked roughly down her body, over the curve of her stomach and into the waistband of her panties. He kept going down, his fingers brushing the soft curls, kept going down to gently part her, feeling her moist and hot on his fingers.

She unwrapped her arms from his neck, her hands meeting his on her own waist. "Get these off," she panted, pulling at the waistband of her underwear. He let her pull them down, shimmy out of them. Then he bent down, one arm on her waist, one arm under her legs, and he tossed her on the bed.

Mal held on to the sheets as she bounced on the bed.

"Did you just throw me?" Her glazed-over expression was slowly being replaced by incredulity. Move fast, Carson.

He would have moved faster if he wasn't distracted by her bouncing breasts. He would have said something funny, some quick retort to show he could match her, wit to wit. But then, talking had never been his strong suit. And, of course, breasts.

Keith crawled across the bed, crawling until he had her trapped underneath him, his knees outside of her thighs, his arms at her shoulders. She reached up to caress his chest, then leaned up to lick his nipples, then to bite. Keith inhaled sharply.

"Sorry!"

"No, oh, God, do that again."

She did. His cock jumped; he was close. Too close, dammit. He leaned away from her, then bent down to give her a deep, deep kiss.

"Mal," he whispered into her mouth, tasting how sweet she was. He moved his lips down her neck, licking the pulse there, feeling how soft she was. She reached between them, trying to touch him.

"No, Mal, I can't."

"Please."

She wouldn't stop, so he grabbed her wrist, then firmly held it over her head. She looked at him, a little shocked, excited. He moved her other wrist up, then held both wrists with one hand. Her breasts were raised high by the movement and he placed wet kisses on each one, slowly savoring her softness. He continued to hold her wrists up and kissed down her body, across her stomach, until——

"No," she said, closing her legs and bringing her knees up.

He looked up, meeting her eyes.

"Please, I don't want to wait."

He didn't want to be accused of being cruel, especially when he was restraining her arms like that. He really didn't want to stop doing that, so he kissed his way back up her body as her legs fell apart, welcoming his hips between them.

"Ready?" he said, nudging her.

"Unh," she said, wrapping her legs around his hips, pulling him closer.

He kept one hand on her wrists and slid one hand under her bottom. She was so soft; he barely registered reaching into his bedside table for a condom before he buried himself in her, moving slowly until his hips met hers. She exhaled, a look of ecstasy on her face.

"OK?"

"Unh," she said, holding him to her with her legs, starting to move her hips upward. He started to move, too, but she said, "No, don't move. Let me."

Mal slid down underneath him, bracing her feet on the bed as she pushed slowly upward. Keith stared down at her with a glazed expression, wanting to move, but she pulled one leg up and wrapped it around his waist. She was straining against his arms. He really, really wanted to move.

"I'll let go of your wrists if you let me move," he panted into her ear.

"Yes, yes, OK," she said frantically. He released her wrists and she entwined them around his back, up over his shoulders. He looked at her, straining against him, moving deliberately, and he shifted against her. They moved together, coming together, backing up until they were nearly separated, coming together again. He couldn't hold back; he increased the pace, and then she was keeping up with him. She clutched his shoulder blades, her nails digging.

"Keith! Keith!" she panted with each pump of his hips. He pumped one more time, hard, shouted her name, and exploded inside of her. She shuddered underneath him, shouting his name right back.

His arms gave out and he collapsed next to her. He looked over at her, her eyes fluttering closed, her lips releasing a sated sigh. "I love you." He sighed, pulling her close to him, placing his hand gently on her head. He fell asleep.

Mal didn't think she had ever been so happily tired in her life. She felt Keith's heavy weight leave her body, and she thought, *Oh, now it's over.* Then he pulled her close. She thought she heard him say, "I love you," but surely not, surely that was some sort of post-coital wishful thinking. Surely he didn't love her, she thought as she buried her head in his chest, feeling his hand come up to cover the back of her head, his other hand running a sleepy caress over her hip. Surely not, she thought, as she fell asleep.

Chapter 21

Mal wasn't exactly sure why she had snuck back into the house at dawn. There was no real reason why she shouldn't spend the morning in Keith's bed, and when she remembered how he'd woken her up in the middle of the night to take her for a third time, her reasons for leaving seemed even more flimsy. Besides, there was no way Miss Libby was not aware of where she'd spent most of the night—or at least where she hadn't spent it.

Still, she woke up just before dawn with an overwhelming feeling of impropriety. Was impropriety even a feeling? Whatever it was, she felt it, and she dressed quickly and snuck out of the bunkhouse.

She managed to sleep for another hour or so, Peanut snoring softly at her feet, running in his sleep. It paled in comparison to what she had just left, but it was better than nothing, she supposed.

She sighed and stretched, feeling gloriously sore, blushing as she remembered what had made her sore. Keith—who would have thought? Strong, silent, and so generous. Loving, even.

She was startled out of that alarming thought by a knock at her bedroom door.

Luke stuck his head in. "Hey, baby, I'm home."

Keith woke up alone, and he woke up hungry, blinking in the sunshine streaming through the curtains. He wasn't sure why Mal had left, and he wasn't looking forward to a confrontation with anyone. Lord help him if Miss Libby thought he'd taken advantage of her. But he hadn't, had he? She wanted him as much as he wanted her. He had felt it all week, a quiet pulse between them. He felt it last night, when she responded to him so warmly. He felt it when they were making love, and when they were holding each other afterward, then again when they were making love, he thought, laughing to himself.

Pushing the thought aside, he headed for the shower—a cold one. He showered, quickly toweled off, threw on his jeans, and ran out into the yard. He thought he would run into the kitchen, find Peanut, then grab some of Miss Libby's breakfast. Instead he ran out and straight into his brother's fist.

"Hey, asshole!"

"Luke, calm down, what—"

Luke punched him in the mouth.

"Luke, what the hell?" He dodged another blow.

"I ought to break your nose, you pervert."

Keith dodged right, then put his own fists up defensively.

"I brought her to this house because I thought she'd be *safe* and you pick that moment to wake the fuck up. No woman's good enough for you, none of the local girls who threw themselves at you, then I bring *one woman* home and you suddenly find yourself!"

"Luke, stop—" Keith grabbed Luke's right arm and wrenched it behind his back, turning him and twisting so Luke was temporarily disarmed. "Calm the hell down!"

"I'm not calming down, you asshole! I'm talking about you getting drunk and taking advantage of a vulnerable woman who, by the way, is engaged to *me*! I'm talking about you living like a goddamn monk, treating everyone like the miserable bastard that you are until you can take someone who belongs to *me*!"

"She doesn't belong to you, Luke."

"You just want her because you can't have her!"

"Keith, please don't hurt him!"

Keith looked up to see Mal running toward them, her face desperate. He wrenched Luke's arm a little harder. Was that what she thought? That he was just taking advantage of an opportunity? Was that what *he* was to *her*? Someone to help her get over her husband? Someone to warm her bed until Luke came home?

Luke took advantage of Keith's momentary confusion to twist himself out of Keith's grip, tearing his shirt in the process. He turned on Keith, swinging his fist hard. Keith ducked, but Mal had gotten herself in between them to stop the fight. Instead *she* stopped Luke's fist. With her face.

They all three stood there stunned, the brothers looking at Mal, Mal staring into the space between them.

Then both men moved at once. Luke reached for Mal, regret in his eyes. Keith grabbed Luke's shirt, pulling him back.

"Don't you dare touch her."

Luke turned on him, tearing his shirt again. His fists came up and he grabbed Keith around the shoulders, trying to pull him down. Keith got a leg under him and kicked out, knocking Luke to the ground. Mal stood there, still stunned.

"Hey! Knock it off, you animals!" Miss Libby shouted as she turned the hose on the boiling men. They looked up, soaked.

"You two ought to be ashamed of yourselves. Don't come inside until you have cooled off. Mal, sweetie, come with me." She grabbed Mal's hand and dragged her, still stunned, into the house.

Keith looked over at his brother, who looked like a wet dog. "You asshole," he said in a low voice.

Luke looked at him helplessly. "Did I punch her in the face?"

Keith nodded, breathing hard.

"Shit. Shit, I'm so sorry," Luke said, looking toward the house.

"It was an accident," Keith said, even though he wanted to pummel his brother into the ground for hurting her.

"You don't understand," Luke started, then punched into the dirt at his feet.

"Luke, you were way out of line, but she'll see—"

"He hit her."

Keith stared at his brother, water dripping onto his forehead.

"That's how I convinced her to leave. He hit her, she came to me, and we left."

A million questions ran through Keith's mind, too fast for any of them to take hold.

"They were separated. Right after I met her, I think. But for months afterward, she still lived with him. We talked about it, she and I, and we'd work out a plan for her to confront him, stand her ground, and move out. We wrote it out, dammit. But every time, he talked her out of it. Every damn time she was back to ironing his goddamn shirts while he screwed other women in their bed."

"How?"

"The way she is now, that's nothing like she was before. When I met her, she would jump at her own shadow. She never did anything without asking Michael's permission first. I wouldn't have seen her again if I didn't work all those stupid charity luncheons she went to."

Keith thought about the way Mal acted after she got off the phone with Michael, how she was always quiet and tentative. The way it took a while for her to get back to herself.

"How often did he hit her?"

"Just the once, according to her. That's enough, don't you think?" Luke finally looked at Keith.

Keith pressed his fist into his forehead. That was more than enough.

"She was trying to sign a lease on an apartment. Some dinky studio. I was cosigning for her. Can you imagine? Anyway, he found it. He thought she was fooling around with me, and he hit her. It was my fault."

"Were you?"

"What, fooling around with her? Jesus, Keith, I'm not an animal."

Keith was starting to feel like *he* was the animal. "It wasn't your fault."

"That's what she said. I'm responsible, Keith. She's my responsibility."

"She can take care of herself now."

Luke sighed. "She said that, too."

"I didn't take advantage of her," Keith said. "I mean, we drank at the Harvest Festival, but nothing really happened until later." Luke didn't need to know about their aborted drunken make-out session. "It wasn't planned, I swear. The more time we spent together, ah, I don't know. I'm not good at this."

"The more time you spent together, the more time you wanted to spend together?"

"Yeah, something like that. Exactly like that."

"Even though you knew we were engaged." The bitter accusation returned to Luke's tone.

"No." Keith gave him his older-brother-knows-best look. "She told us pretty early on that your engagement was fake. What the hell were you thinking? What kind of game were *you* playing with her?"

"It wasn't a game." Luke looked up when Keith snorted. "Fine, but it wasn't that kind of game. I wasn't tricking her. She needed to get away, and this seemed like a good plan."

"Pretending to be engaged to a stranger seemed like a good plan?"

"We weren't strangers, Keith. We were friends. We *are* friends."

"I tried to stay away," Keith said.

"But, what, she pounced on you?"

"Watch it."

"Keith, I've never seen you think with anything but your head before. What the hell are you doing, starting something with this woman?"

"I don't know."

"Is she just a fling? Or are you going to make a go for it? Are you going to ask her to live here? On a goddamn failing horse farm? Do you know what her life was like in DC, Keith? She had everything she wanted. Here, we don't even have an extra car for her to borrow. How are you going to take care of her?"

Keith kicked his shoe in the dirt. "Mal can take care of herself."

"She can? Then what the hell does she need you for?"

Keith looked up, not knowing the answer. It was then he noticed the beat-up chrome horse trailer parked next to the stable.

"What's that?"

Luke smiled. "It's an investment."

"Luke . . ."

"Keith, it's a sure thing. This stud horse was going for auction, and he's a beauty."

"We're not set up for that."

"But we can be. Look, we'll talk about it later, when Dad's here."

"And Katie."

"Damn, Katie's going to hate it. Maybe I can get Chase to talk to her. Or Mal—does she get along with Mal?"

"Yeah. Everybody does."

"She's a sweet girl. That's a warning, Keith."

Keith sighed, ran his fingers through his hair. "I won't hurt her. I don't know what I'm doing here. I should just leave her be."

"Is that what you want?"

"Sure, yes." Keith paused, looked up over toward the cottage he should have been sharing with his wife. "Is that what you want me to do?"

"I love that girl, Keith. I would do anything for her."

Keith looked at his little brother, sitting in the wet dirt.

"When I went to her room this morning, she was bouncing off the walls, telling me all the stuff she's been doing around here. Did you know she really likes filing?"

Keith laughed. "It's a sickness."

"You guys have been good for her."

"You think?"

"Why do you think I brought her here?"

"I think you brought her here because you had no other options."

"Can we just pretend, for once, that one of my ideas is working out the way I planned?"

Keith clapped him on the shoulder. "Yeah, fine. We'll pretend."

They stood up and looked toward the house.

"Keith?"

"Yeah?"

"Make sure you stay good for her, or I'll hit you for real."

Chapter 22

When Keith and Luke came in through the back kitchen door, tails between their legs, they were greeted by a disapproving scowl from Miss Libby and the sight of Mal sitting at the counter with a frozen steak on her face.

"Sweetheart, I'm so sorry——" Mal held up a hand before Luke could finish.

"I've had it. I'm tired, I'm cranky, and my head hurts. I'm sick of men. I'm sick of your power trips and your fighting. I'm done with men! Miss Libby, run away with me."

Miss Libby laughed. "You're too young for me, but it's a lovely offer." Her look turned disapproving the second she turned back to the brothers. "You two, I'm not sure about. I'm tempted to send you to your rooms without your supper."

Keith's attention, though, was on Mal. "Does your head hurt?"

She gave him a one-eyed glare. "What do you think?"

"Can I look at it?" At her skeptical glance, he said, "I'm a doctor. I mean, I know I'm a vet, but please let me look at your face."

She lowered the steak and he kneeled down in front of her. "Follow my finger." She did. He gingerly touched the tender skin around her eye. She flinched. It was already starting to bruise. "How bad is your headache?"

"It's nothing." She looked at Luke, who had started to protest. "I'm not just being stoic here. My eye is throbbing a little, but my brain does not feel jarred."

"Mal," Keith said softly. "Luke told me that Michael——"

Mal snapped her head toward Luke, then winced.

"Should we take her to the hospital?" Luke was nervously pacing the linoleum.

Keith gave her an assessing look. "No, I think she's fine. We'll just keep an eye on her tonight."

Luke stepped forward and reached for her hand. "Mal, I'm so—"

"Don't," she said, taking her hand back and returning the steak to her face. "I know it was an accident. I accept your apology. I stepped into your fist, which was a stupid thing for me to do." She stood up, touched Luke gently on the shoulder. "It's not the same thing."

"Baby——"

Mal turned back to Keith. "But I still hate both of you, and if I see you fighting again, especially over me, I'll make sure Miss Libby never cooks for you again."

"And I won't," Miss Libby agreed.

Just then, Cal walked into the kitchen. "Why is Mal wearing my dinner on her face?"

Chapter 23

Keith wouldn't let Mal take a nap—he wanted to be able to keep an eye on her in case there was any residual head damage. But no one else in the family—Keith included—would let her lift a hand to do anything. It was like when she first arrived, although this was worse because now she knew what she could do. She tried helping Libby in the kitchen, only to be shooed away into the living room. She didn't want to see Keith. She couldn't handle the concern and pity she saw in his eyes where she used to see desire. She tried to help Chase in the barn even though what she knew about horses she could fit into a thimble. Chase gamely showed her how the mares liked to be brushed and she was getting along just fine until Katie caught them at it.

"Mal! What are you doing!"

Mal dropped the brush guiltily as if she had been caught with a joint instead of a horse brush.

"Relax, Katie. She's just brushing Lucy."

"She's supposed to be resting!"

"But I'm not allowed to sleep!"

"Well, she shouldn't be around the horses," Katie yelled at Chase, ignoring Mal. "She could get hurt! What if one of them bolts or something!"

"First of all, they're not going to bolt if they have nothing to provoke them—and you coming in here yelling like the house is on fire is definitely going to provoke them. Secondly, she's brushing *Lucy*, who is deaf and half blind. That horse wouldn't bolt if you kicked her."

Mal put a protective hand on Lucy's rump, trying not to feel insulted that she was just being humored with this task. She had thought she was being helpful.

"Well, she's done here. I need her in the house."

"Um, hi. Do I get any say in this?"

Chase and Katie turned from where they were arguing toe-to-toe and looked at her, as if seeing her for the first time.

"I got punched in the face—by accident, I know. I'm not crippled or mentally incapacitated. I can brush a half-dead horse, dammit."

Katie looked at her sympathetically. "I know, I'm sorry. Luke feels terrible and he's beating himself up and driving me up the wall. Dad's taking it out on this 'investment idea' of Luke's. Did you see that horse?" she asked Chase.

"He's a beauty."

"I hate to admit it, and if you ever say I did I will deny it, but I think Luke might have done good here."

"We'll see what your father says."

Katie snorted. "Well, right about now he's not going to say anything Luke wants to hear."

Mal threw up her hands. "Luke has nothing to be sorry about on my account. Really! It was an accident. He should be sorry that he was acting like a Neanderthal—so should Keith—but I don't hold this against him."

"It's a pretty good shiner," Chase said helpfully. Katie gave him a jab in the ribs. "Well, it is!"

"The only good thing about it is that it's going to make the two of them feel like crap every time they look at you, which they should," Katie said.

"Great, that's just the boost my self-confidence needs."

"Sorry. I'm a vengeful little sister. Listen, I have to run into town so I'll take you to the library. You can use Luke's library card and rack up all kinds of fines for him."

When they got back, Mal sat on the porch, wrapped in a blanket, sipping tea and reading trashy books with one eye, holding an ice pack over the other. She'd been planning to check out something serious and smart-looking, but in the end, she decided she would get what she really wanted. Luckily, the gray-haired librarian in sensible shoes knew just what she was looking for: a happy ending.

As she followed one woman's journey from kick-ass bounty hunter to happily alpha after, she thought about her own closure.

Maybe it was remembering Keith's hairy chest, but more likely it was the throbbing of her swollen eye, getting better by the minute. What was she doing here? Hiding out from Michael? Hadn't she learned to stand on her own two feet? She could face Michael now, right?

Only one way to find out.

She snuck the cordless phone to the porch and dialed her old home number. She would have preferred to use her cell, but, well, that was pretty much out of order. The line rang and rang, and she was just debating whether or not to leave a message when Michael picked up.

"Hello?" He sounded like he was just waking up.

"Michael?"

"Who is this?"

"Michael, it's Mal. Mallory."

"Oh, my wife," he spat.

"Who is that?" she heard a female voice in the background.

"It's my goddamn wife," he shouted, not entirely away from the mouthpiece.

"Well, tell her you're busy and come back to bed!"

Ugh, thought Mal. *The sooner this is over, the better.*

"Mallory, I have to go. Busy."

"Michael, wait a second. I want to talk to you."

"You finally want to talk? What do you want?"

"I'm coming home. We need to get divorced."

It wasn't until about half an hour before dinner that Keith realized he hadn't seen Mal all afternoon. Remembering how she had followed him that first morning on the farm, begging for something to do, he was a little surprised. But then, Luke had punched her in the face, no matter how accidentally. *Unlike her husband*, he thought, clenching his fists. Any man who would hit a woman in anger didn't deserve . . .

But Michael wasn't here. Mal was. Maybe she was passed out somewhere, concussed and suffering. Probably not—if her symptoms had been that bad, Keith would have insisted that she go to the hospital. But it gave him an excuse to find her, and it explained the nervous feeling in the pit of his stomach.

He knew she was mad—not that she got hit, which killed him. He didn't like the way she so easily took the blame. She seemed more mad that they were fighting because of her—as if that was also her responsibility. They weren't really fighting over her—well, they were, but what was there to be so mad about? He and Luke beat each other up all the time; it was how they worked out their problems. Or at least it had been when they were kids. What did Mal mean, that it was about power trips?

He thought he might know, which was the real reason for the nervous stomach. He hated to think of the kind of relationship that she was used to, that she was expecting. Didn't she know him at all? He didn't want power over her. He didn't want to own her. He just wanted a chance to love her.

He finally tracked her down in Luke's old room. She had her suitcase on the bed and she was throwing clothes into it, mumbling to herself. If the force she was using on the clothes was any indication, she was still mad.

He stood in the doorway and cleared his throat.

She turned. No, she whirled on him with fire in her eyes.

Definitely still mad.

"I'm fine, Keith. You don't need to check up on me."

"I'm not."

"Then what do you want?"

Keith paused, rubbed the back of his neck. "To make sure you were OK."

Mal threw a pair of socks into the suitcase.

"Are you going somewhere?" Great, Keith. Very observant.

She gave him a look that said just that.

"I'm going back to DC."

"What? Are you sure that's safe?" He reached for her, but she backed up, away from him.

"Michael is happy with his new girlfriend. It's in his best interests that he get rid of me, and as long as he's getting his way, it's fine. What else am I supposed to do, Keith?" She looked at him, pleading.

He didn't have an answer. Except: *stay*.

"I'm just going for a little while. Michael has the divorce papers ready. I'm going to sign them."

Relief washed over Keith. She would be free. "Then what?"

Mal sighed. "Then, I don't know. I'll just get a job somewhere and start over."

"You have a job here."

Mal raised her eyebrow. "Dr. Monroe will be fine without me. I made sure Billie understands the new system. They don't need me."

"They do need you! What if something happens! What if . . . the computer breaks!" Keith knew he was pleading, and that he was pleading for the wrong things, but he couldn't stop.

"Keith——" She came over to him now, put her hands on his chest. "Let's be honest. There's nothing for me here, is there?"

He looked into her eyes. He thought he saw hope and desire, but maybe that was just her excitement at starting her life over. He couldn't ask her to stay here. He thought about what Luke had said, about her life with Michael. Keith knew he was the better man, but was that enough? He lived in a bunkhouse, for crying out loud. His dog didn't even have four legs. What kind of life could he offer her here?

He ran his finger along the short hair framing her face, then turned and walked out of the room. *Let her go,* he thought. *She doesn't belong here.*

Chapter 24

"We planning on waiting on those girls for dinner?" Since Cal was already seated with his napkin in his lap, he clearly wasn't.

"Katie is driving Mal to the train station. I'm saving her a plate."

Cal grunted. And that was about the end of conversation for the rest of dinner. Libby tried to make small talk, but one look from Cal silenced her. Chase looked like he wished he had decided to eat dinner anywhere else, or that he could resist Libby's cooking. Keith kept his head down, barely tasting the pork chops. Even Luke was unusually silent.

Finally, when Cal was finished, he wiped his mouth with his napkin and looked at Luke. "So, Son, what kind of trouble did you bring us this time?"

Luke, Chase, and Cal headed out to the barn while Keith helped Libby in the kitchen. He didn't want to sit through Cal running Luke over the coals. He knew if Luke's idea was sound, and if it wasn't too expensive, Cal would eventually come around. Maybe. Chase seemed to like the idea of a stud farm. Let Chase invest in it, then.

"What is Luke up to, bringing that stud horse around here?" Libby asked, handing Keith a pot to dry.

"Same thing he always does. Acting without thinking," Keith replied.

"Worked out okay last time," Libby said.

"The topless horseback riding lessons?"

"Good Lord, no," Libby said, laughing. "I thought your father was going to have a heart attack over that one. No, Keith, I meant Mal."

"Yeah, that worked out great."

"She did us all some good, and you know it."

Keith concentrated on getting the pot very, very dry.

"She did you some good, Keith."

He didn't know what to say. He didn't want to admit it was true.

"Why did you let her go, Keith?"

"I didn't *let* her go. She wanted to go, and she went."

"She would have stayed. Or she would have come back. For you. She fit in here, Keith. She worked with you."

Keith looked at Miss Libby, the woman who'd raised him from a lost boy without a mother. "I couldn't ask her to stay. I couldn't do that to her."

Libby patted his hand. "Oh, my sweet boy." They heard shouts coming from the barn. The negotiations were going well, then. "We better go out there and make sure they don't kill each other."

The ride to the train station had been tense and silent, Katie staring straight at the road, Mal looking out the window, trying to memorize the scenery. She would never see it again.

"So you're just going to sign the papers?"

Mal looked over at Katie, who kept her gaze forward. "Yeah."

"He couldn't mail them?"

"Well, sure he could. But you don't know my husband. He's not real big on going out of his way to make things convenient for others."

"If he's such a jerk, why did you marry him?"

"He wasn't always." Mal sighed. "Yes, he was. I was just young and stupid. And then I was too scared to leave. I thought I had invested everything in my marriage, and if I gave it up, I would have nothing left."

Katie took her eyes off the road for a second to look at Mal. "I'm never getting married."

Mal laughed. "I'm pretty sure any marriage of yours will be different from mine."

"Why? You think I can't be married?"

"No, I think you're not going to let a man boss you around."

"That's for damn sure." Katie paused.

"That's not how marriage always is, Katie. Just don't marry an asshole."

Katie snorted. "Well, then there's no danger of me getting married."

They rode in silence for a few more minutes until Katie turned into the train station parking lot. There were a few people milling around in business casual, working their smart phones. They still had a few minutes before the train boarded, and Mal would be gone.

Katie got out and tugged Mal's suitcase out of the backseat. "Well, good luck on your divorce."

"Thanks."

"Are you going to get any money out of it?"

"I doubt it. I don't even care anymore."

"Where are you going to go next?"

"Anywhere, I guess. One step at a time, though."

"I would think you would have more of a plan."

Mal laughed. "Yeah, me, too."

"You could come back here. We can use your help."

Mal snorted. "Sure, I was a real help."

"OK, you're crap at farm work. But we'd love to have you. Keith would, I'm sure."

Mal looked toward the track. The rumble of the train sounded in the distance. Almost time to go. "I'm not so sure about that. If he did, he didn't say."

Katie turned Mal's shoulders so they were face-to-face. "When have you ever known my brother to speak up?"

Mal smiled, pushing down the lump in her throat. She hadn't known Keith long, but she felt that she knew him well. "Train's here."

"You need help up to the platform?" Katie asked.

"No, I'm OK. Thanks for everything." Mal gave her a hug, then lugged her suitcase up to the platform. She fingered the ticket in her pocket. This was it. On to the rest of her life.

When Keith and Libby reached the barn, Luke was shouting in his father's face, waving his arms madly. Chase was stepping in between them. Cal's face was red as a beet, and he was giving Luke a death glare. Then, suddenly, he stepped back and clutched his arm. "Cal?" Libby shouted, hurrying over.

"It's nothing. Indigestion. I'm going to walk it off."

"Keith, walk with your father."

"Dammit, woman, I'm fine! I don't need a babysitter! It's your cooking that's killing me!"

"Fine! Go! Walk! I'll just keep quiet and pick up after you!"

"Good! That's your job!"

Keith, Luke, and Chase all looked at Cal with open-mouthed astonishment. Nobody had ever, not in the twenty years she had worked there, talked to Miss Libby like that. She was their Libby, their mother hen. Nobody ever spoke crossly to her, especially not Cal.

Miss Libby didn't say anything, just turned and walked toward the house.

"Lib, I didn't mean it——"

"Calvin Carson, I have lived with you for twenty years and I have never been made to feel like anything less than part of this family. You take that walk around your damn yard by your own damn self, and then maybe we'll see if I've cooled off enough to accept your apology."

Cal got up and started toward her even as she turned her back on him. He took a few steps, clutched his arm, and collapsed in the dirt.

"Dad!" Luke screamed and ran to his side.

"Oh my God, is he breathing?"

"Call nine-one-one! Libby, get the phone!"

"Let me through! Let me see him!" Keith pushed past Luke and rolled Cal over onto his back, listening for a heartbeat. Without a word, he reared up and began chest compressions. He vaguely heard Chase on the phone with emergency services, and out of the corner of his eye, he saw Luke holding Miss Libby up. Peanut barked from the porch. He only partially registered all that, though, and concentrated on keeping his father alive.

As the train pulled into the station, Mal turned to look for Katie in the parking lot to get one more glimpse of a Carson before she left them all forever. Katie was holding her cell phone to her ear, an intense look on her face—anger? Pain? Mal couldn't figure it out. Then she heard Katie scream "No!" and double over.

Mal left her suitcase and ran back to Katie.

Chapter 25

Mal pulled into the visitor's parking lot. Katie was out of the car before she even put it in park. Mal had to jog to keep up with her, blinking her eyes against the setting sun. Mal was feeling emotionally drained, exhausted from her decision to leave and then propping Katie up after she got the phone call. She had seen Katie's severe moods before, her hot temper and her boisterous laughter, but it scared her to see Katie so destroyed. It had taken Mal a few minutes to get the whole story, but as soon as she heard "Dad" and "hospital," Mal grabbed the car keys. A railway employee had witnessed the scene and brought her bag down to the car. Mal got directions to the hospital and drove.

Katie was obviously not thinking clearly because she walked through the double sliding electric doors of the hospital, then just stood there blinking in the fluorescent light. "Where do I go?" she asked, panic in her voice.

"I'll find out," Mal said, taking Katie's hand and leading her to the reception desk.

They were directed to intensive care. Mal had enough experience with hospitals to know where the waiting room would be, and that they would get no answers before they got there. No use beating up the receptionist, as Katie seemed inclined to do. She squeezed Katie's hand. "Let's find your family."

Katie grunted in acknowledgement, but she held on to Mal's hand for dear life, her palms sweating.

They walked into the waiting room. There were a few other families there, looking up hopefully, then quickly back down to reexamine months-old magazines when they saw Mal and Katie weren't there for them. Chase came over and wrapped Katie in a hug, whispering in her ear as she broke down.

Mal looked away, wanting to give them space. She headed toward Luke and Miss Libby, who held out her hand to Mal. "Thank God you're here," she said. Mal thought that was a funny thing to say; she'd just brought Katie. She didn't belong here.

"How is Cal?"

"The doctor said he's fine, resting. We haven't been able to see him yet. Keith's talking to the doctor now."

As if on cue, Keith walked around the corner and immediately met her eye. He stopped, looking confused. "Mal," he said, dumbly.

"I brought Katie."

Keith looked over at Katie and Chase coming toward him, Chase's arm tight around Katie's shoulders. She untangled herself and Keith gave her an only slightly awkward hug. Keith put a hand on the back of Luke's neck. "He's been asking for you."

"Shit, Keith, what happened?"

"Heart attack."

Miss Libby paled and grabbed Mal's hand.

"He's fine," Keith said to Miss Libby. "I mean, he's not fine, he had a heart attack. He's recovering. I was able to see him. Libby, don't worry, he's definitely waking up."

"How mean was he?"

"Tired and weak, but mean as a snake."

"Oh, thank God!" She broke down in relieved tears.

The Carsons stood around uncomfortably, not knowing how to comfort Libby—the tables were usually turned and she was the one comforting.

"I just kept thinking about how we fought, and how those could not be the last words we ever said to each other."

"Well, you can go in and see him now and say whatever you want to him."

Miss Libby stood. "Good. I'm going to kill him."

After a long, long night, Cal passed the critical phase. As the sun started to rise, he was out of the woods. The doctors wanted to keep him at least one more day for tests and observation, but since the ward limited visitors to two at a time, the Carsons decided to split up. Luke came and took Miss Libby's hand. She patted his cheek affectionately, and she and Katie walked back to the waiting room.

"I don't want to go yet," Luke said to Keith.

"I'll go back and check on things at home."

"Come on, Luke, I'll buy you breakfast and bring you back," Chase said.

Keith and Mal stood alone in the hallway. Keith seemed to be staring a hole through her.

"Um, I guess I'll go," she said, avoiding his eyes. She didn't know where she would go, but she couldn't really stay here.

"Thank you for coming."

"I just drove Katie."

"You really helped, Mal. Libby was glad to see you."

"Well, I know hospitals." She gave a weak laugh.

"Right."

They stood, staring like dopes. Mal found, now that she was back, she didn't want to go again.

"Mal?"

"Hmm?"

"I know you were planning on . . ."

"Getting divorced?"

"Yeah," Keith rubbed his neck. "And, of course, I want you to do that. I mean, I want you to do what you need to do. But . . ."

"What, Keith?"

"I hate to ask you this."

"Ask, Keith."

"We could really use you. If you can stay."

Mal sighed. "I can stay."

Chapter 26

They didn't have much conversation on the way home. Keith drove. Mal contented herself watching the scenery go by, again. Winter was coming fast, and the trees were losing their leaves. It still looked beautiful to her.

Keith parked in front of the bunkhouse, and Peanut came charging out to the truck. He pounced on Mal when she opened the door, tail wagging maniacally. "Hey, boy, did you miss me?" Mal asked, rubbing his ears. Peanut jumped up on her chest and, as usual, Mal wasn't ready and she landed on her butt in the dirt.

Mal laughed and accepted Keith's hand up. "Well, at least someone's glad to see me."

Keith looked at her. "You think I'm not glad to see you?"

"No, Keith. That's not what I meant——"

"Do you really think you mean nothing to me?"

"No." *Yes,* Mal thought. "No, of course not."

"What kind of person does it make me that I feel grateful my dad just had a heart attack because it brought you back to me?"

Mal gasped. "I had no idea. Keith——"

"Forget it," he turned to go into the barn.

"No! Keith, I won't——" She grabbed his arm and pulled him to her. He was on her in an instant, his mouth hot and insistent.

Mal put her hands on his chest to push away, to slow him down, step back, talk about it. But then his lips descended on hers again, and she felt that comfortable warm pressure of his lips, growing less comfortable and more insistent as he teased her mouth open, tasting her with his tongue.

She forgot what she was supposed to talk to him about. Was it

something about slowing down? Surely she didn't have any reason
to slow this down.

"Mal," Keith said, coming up for air, then leaving slow, urgent
kisses down her neck, walking her into the barn. "I want you."

"Yes," she whispered. His head shot up, his eyes locking with
hers. Suddenly, he tightened his grip around her waist and hoisted
her up. She gasped as the air was squeezed out of her, but she
wrapped her legs around his waist, finding a secure mooring there,
not to mention creating a delicious tension against his crotch. He
started walking, slowly and with some difficulty, toward the couch
in the small living area. As he kicked the door closed behind him,
he vaguely heard Peanut's mournful whimper outside the door, but
he didn't care. Mal was clinging to his neck, her gorgeous thighs
wrapped around his waist, and she was kissing him back with as
much ferocity as he was kissing her.

He was so caught up in their battle of tongues that he missed the
little coffee table he had set up in his half-assed attempt at decorat-
ing, and he tumbled onto the couch. He caught himself before he
landed on Mal, and she lay there, a bit dazed by the hard landing.

"Sorry, dammit, sorry. Are you OK?"

"I think being around you is bad for my health. I seem to keep
getting injured."

"Oh, God, I'm sorry, are you hurt? Show me where it hurts."

She pushed him back so he was sitting next to her on the couch,
then she swung one leg up and straddled him. She put a finger on
her neck, right at her pulse point.

"Here."

He placed a kiss there, licking her pulse a little.

"Here," she said, unbuttoning the top button of her blouse, pointing to the cleft between her breasts. He kissed her there.

"Here?" he asked as she unbuttoned her shirt farther, cupping her
breasts through the lace of her bra.

"Mmm-hmm," she said, her eyes bright. "Both sides."

He gave equal attention to each breast, pulling at the nipple
through the lace of her bra, then, when she unhooked the front clasp,
he tasted each one straight on. He urged her closer to him and she
complied, wiggling her hips against him in pleasure.

"Mal," he warned, a little breathless.

"I want you, too." She looked into his eyes, and his heart constricted. This was the first time she'd admitted that she wanted him, the first time she'd said it out loud. God, he thought. He really did love this woman.

She reached between them and undid the fastenings to her jeans. He thought that was a great idea, so he did the same for his own. He eased her jeans down over her hips, stopping at her knees. The action caught her off-balance and she tipped forward. He took advantage of the close proximity of her beautiful breasts to take another taste. "So sweet," he murmured.

She reached for him, gently pulling his hard length out of his jeans. He lifted his hips up so she could move his jeans down a little. Then she took him in hand, firmly stroking him from root to tip. He reached around behind her, his rough hands running over her smooth skin, and he found her center, wet and ready for him. He inserted one finger, then two. She gasped and wiggled on him a little more, tightening her grip on his cock.

He removed his hand and she sighed. Then he reached up to cup her neck, urging her forward for a deep soul kiss. She responded in kind, their tongues hungry and clashing, and she inched forward on his lap. He positioned himself at her entrance, then broke the kiss and looked into her eyes. She placed her hands on either side of his head, stroking his hair. He reached into his back pocket and pulled out a condom. She looked as if she wanted to ask why he had it there, but stopped as she took it from him, rolled it down. She bit her lower lip as he started to enter her, letting her head fall back as he entered her fully. He kissed the creamy expanse of her neck; she really was sweet. They both started to move, he thrust up, she moaned in pleasure, then rocked her hips forward as much as she could, constrained as she was by her jeans around her knees. They found their rhythm quickly, as if they were old hat and not new, frenzied lovers. He tightened his arms around her waist and buried his face in her breasts. She tugged at his hair, first pulling his face closer to her breasts, then pulling him up for a kiss. He wanted to kiss her and kiss her, to kiss her while she came. She was frantic in her rhythm, trying to move faster, rocking her hips harder. He tilted his hips up, receiving a shocked moan for the new spot he was hitting, then worked a hand between their bodies. He stroked her as they rocked, and she broke the kiss, screaming his name as they shuddered together.

She collapsed on top of him, her arms around his neck. He inhaled her sweet scent, satisfied, and rubbed his hands up and down her back, not ready to stop touching her yet. When he moved up to her neck, she sighed as he kneaded the muscles there.

"You're tense."

"I know," she said into his shoulder. He kissed her neck and tried to nudge her head up, but she burrowed farther into his neck, tightening her thighs around his waist. "Not yet! I'm not ready yet."

He let her sit there on his lap, holding him with her whole body, until she was ready.

Finally she moved a little, without fully getting up. "OK, my legs are starting to cramp." He gently withdrew himself from her, lifting her off his lap. She righted her clothes and watched as he did the same.

She looked a little lost, so he pulled her back down to the couch, next to him this time, and put his arm around her shoulder. She sighed, wrapped her arms around his waist and rested her head on his shoulder.

"What am I going to do with you, Mal?" he said, stroking her hair gently back from her face.

"Well, what you just did was pretty nice."

"Pretty nice?"

"Mind blowing!" she said, laughing.

He continued to stroke her hair. "I'm falling in love with you." He felt her tense up. He tilted her chin so he was looking in her eyes. "We'll talk about it later. We have work to do."

They spent the afternoon working, sometimes separately, sometimes together. Keith gave her projects to do in the barn and she spent a few exhausting hours mucking, brushing horses, cleaning tack. Keith called the hospital, but nobody was ready to leave. Cal was awake and recovering, but would have to stay one more night. Mal raided Libby's kitchen and put together sandwiches and pasta salad and Keith drove it over to the hospital. Mal enjoyed playing house (and, truthfully, enjoyed having free rein in the usually forbidden kitchen), so she pulled bits and pieces together and made a casserole for dinner. She always felt hopeless in the kitchen with Michael—nothing she cooked seemed to turn out right—but she liked the idea of feeding Keith. When they sat down to eat, she was not disappointed. He scarfed down three big servings, and a large bowl of the ice cream he had brought home for dessert. Later, he showed his appreciation for her culinary care by lighting a fire in the bunkhouse's fireplace. Then he sat her down and rubbed her shoulders until she was drowsy with fatigue and relaxation. He led her to the bedroom and peeled off their clothes. As soon as he lay down with her, though, his own exhaustion hit. He pulled her close, and fell asleep.

Mal watched Keith sleep for a while. He was not a particularly cute sleeper—he had an iron grip around her shoulders, and his head was thrown back with his mouth open. She was surprised at how quiet his snoring was. He was so surprising. He was falling in love with her, he had said. Was that what she was feeling? Was that why her heart sped up when she looked at him? Why she had this need to take care of him? Why she wanted to lay everything bare, let him see all of her? Was that because he loved her, or because she loved him?

She wriggled out from under his arm. Keith moaned and rolled over, but he let her go. She pulled on his flannel shirt, loving how it came halfway down her thighs. He really was a big guy. But she had more important things to do than moon over Keith, so she slipped on her boots and tiptoed out to the office.

While Keith went to the hospital, she had called Michael to let him know that she hadn't made her train. He hadn't picked up, so she'd left him a message. She was a little surprised that she hadn't heard from him—Michael was not great when he didn't get his way, nor was he great at thinking before he acted. She spent the evening expecting the phone to ring. But, no. Well, if this was a power trip to make her stew, it was working. She wanted a divorce; she needed closure more than ever. This new confession of Keith's gave the divorce an urgency she hadn't felt before. She had wanted to be done with Michael so she could move on. But now she was starting to feel a direction she wanted to go in, and she was anxious to get started.

It was late, but Michael worked irregular hospital hours. At least she thought he did; now she wasn't sure how many of those late nights were really spent romancing other doctors' wives. That didn't matter anymore; she was done feeling rejected by Michael. But she did hope that he was still going home after work.

She dialed, then released the breath she didn't realize she was holding when the answering machine picked up. "Hi, Michael. It's Mallory. I hope you got my earlier message about missing the train. I'm not sure when I'm going to be able to make it out there, but I do want to sign those papers. Give me a call at this number. I should be around tomorrow." She thought about how Michael must have reacted when she hadn't responded to his summons to return to DC. "Thanks so much for being patient with me. I know you're busy." She sighed. Did that sound as fake as it felt? "OK, talk to you tomorrow."

She hung up and looked around the office. It really was a mess in here. The file cabinet was more stacked than filed. She shuffled a few of the piles on the desk, trying to make sense of them. Usually, even in a mess, she could find the system—pending bills, invoices to mail, purchase orders. This—there was no order she could see. It was driving her crazy, and, conveniently, shuffling papers would be a good distraction from thinking about Michael. Keith wouldn't mind, would he?

She picked up a pile of invoices to sort them by date, but as she lifted them, she knocked over the massive pile of papers underneath. "Damn," she said, and bent down to gather them up.

"This is the weirdest sex dream I've ever had in my life."

Mal squeaked and jumped up. Keith was standing behind her in his jeans and his unlaced boots. His hair was ruffled and he had a pillow mark on his cheek.

"What?"

"This must be a dream. Why else would you be practically naked in my office?"

"I couldn't sleep."

"So you thought you would organize?"

"It relaxes me."

"I know." He came over to her and put his hands on her waist. "You are very strange."

She wrapped her arms around his back as his mouth came down on her neck. "You need to know that about me if I'm going to stay."

"You'll stay?"

"I want to. I can't get hold of Michael, but as soon as I do, I'll be a free woman."

Keith sat down on the desk chair. "I'm glad."

"Good," she said, approaching him.

He held up a hand. "Mal, I need to know what happened."

She wanted to pretend that she didn't know what he was talking about. She wanted to live the rest of her life never having to tell anyone about the humiliating night when she'd let her husband smack her around.

She fingered the new bruise under her eye, already fading.

"Please." Keith said, leaning forward so his elbows rested on his knees.

She looked at him, at the warm green of his eyes, the firm set of his jaw. If this was going to work, he had to know all of her.

"It only happened once," she started. Keith clasped his hands together in front of him, his knuckles white. "We had been separated for a while. Not very long yet; I was still living with him. I was delusional enough to think that was just temporary until I could find a place."

She gave a little laugh and looked down at her hands.

"So I did. I found a place advertised in the paper. I don't know how I thought I was going to pay for it; I didn't even have a job yet. Actually, Luke was talking to his boss to see if I could work for her." She looked up at Keith. "Can you imagine? I would have been a terrible waitress."

"I think you're good at anything you set your mind to."

He really believed that, she thought. What a strange sensation, to know someone believed in her.

"Well, anyway, it wouldn't have been very fun, serving people who used to be my friends. But it was better than nothing."

"Michael didn't like that?" Keith asked when it looked as though she would stop talking.

"Oh, no. He definitely didn't like that," she said, her eyes misting over. Dammit, hadn't she cried over him enough?

"Mal." Keith started to get up, but Mal held out a hand to still him.

"Let me finish. Let me say this before I chicken out." She took a deep breath. "He didn't like it. He found the lease that Luke had cosigned. Stupid me, I left it out so I would remember to drop it off at the rental agency. He found it, and he freaked out. No wife of his would shack up with a worthless bartender." She waved her arms and raised her voice in imitation of Michael's anger. "No wife of his would make a fool of him, running around town with some piece of meat." She laughed, and a tear escaped and ran down her cheek. "That was Luke, the piece of meat."

"Got it."

"So I said, 'What do you care? We're not even married any-more!'" She wiped her cheek, but the tears wouldn't stop. She knew how this story ended. "Keep in mind that we're having this argument while there is a nurse upstairs sleeping in our bed. In his bed. Yes, it's true. I married a doctor who seduces nurses. It gets better and better, doesn't it?"

She was frantic now, pacing back and forth in the small space. Keith kept still in his chair, his hands locked in front of him.

"So I said, 'What do you care? We're not married!' And he said, 'We're married until I say we're not married. You can't just run around like a slut! You're my wife!' And I said, 'Why not? He makes me feel better than you ever could! You're half the man he is!'"

Keith looked up.

"I don't know why I said that," Mal continued, not meeting Keith's eye. "I never slept with Luke. I had never even *kissed* him, or thought about him as anything other than a friend. I shouldn't have said that to Michael. It wasn't right."

"You were mad."

"I was livid. All those years of doing whatever he wanted, whenever he wanted, and now he wasn't even going to let me go. I snapped. I shouldn't have said that about Luke, but I got what I wanted. Michael reacted."

"He hit you."

"Right in the face. I provoked him. I shouldn't have provoked him."

"He shouldn't have fucking hit you."

Mal finally looked over at Keith. She felt the tension coming off his shoulders in waves. He would never hit her, no matter what she said to him. She could feel his anger, and his disgust. It was what she was most afraid of, telling him this story. But she saw that his disgust was not aimed at her, but at Michael, at a man so weak that he could not control his temper. She understood that this was how Keith saw it, without his having to say anything. She understood him, and she knew where she stood with him. She always had.

It scared her silly. She sat on the edge of the desk.

"He shouldn't have hit me. But he did. And I can't say I'm glad that he did, but I do wonder if he hadn't, whether I would still be living there. Or whether I would have eventually found a way out. But if he hadn't, I wouldn't have come to Luke, and he wouldn't have brought me here. So, in a way, I'm grateful."

Keith stood, closed the distance between them in two strides. He cupped her cheek in his hand and ran a finger under her eye, where Luke's bruise was fading. "It wasn't your fault that he hit you."

She looked up at him, and startled tears began to run down her face again. "I provoked him. I shouldn't have said that stuff about Luke."

Keith kissed her cheek, gently, softly. "It doesn't matter what you said. He was wrong to hit you, and that's not your fault."

She shook her head, pursing her lips together to keep from sobbing. "It was my fault."

"No," Keith said. He gathered her in his arms, tucked her head against his warm chest, and gently rocked her back and forth while she wept. He had time to convince her that she was not to blame. He would take it.

When she was cried out, he pulled her face up to look at her. "I am grateful for my brother, though. I'm glad as hell he was there for you, and I'm glad he came up with this harebrained scheme to bring you here."

"Even though we were lying to you?"

"I'll get over it."

"I'm glad Luke brought me here, too," Mal said, tracing the fine hair on his chest.

"Yeah?"

"Yeah. I'm even thinking about staying."

Keith pulled her hand away and held it tight. "Before you commit to anything, Mal, you should know that I lied to you, too."

Mal pulled back. "What?"

Keith pulled her back to him. "I lied yesterday. I'm not falling in love with you. I am in love with you. Maybe from the moment I first saw you, when I thought you were with Luke. I don't know if you realize what you do to me. I thought that part of me was closed forever. I don't really know what to do about it. But I do know that I want you to be here, with me."

Mal looked at him, blinking as the tears spilled over her lashes.

"Oh, no, don't cry. Please, baby. Not over me."

"I think that's the most you've ever said to me the whole time we've known each other."

He kissed her gently. "Should I stop talking?"

"Well, I like what you're saying."

"Yeah?"

"Yeah. I want to be here with you. I want to see if this can work."

He kissed her again, pulling her close against his chest. He ran his hands up her back, then cupped her face, pouring all of his love into the kiss. He wanted to show her more, though, so he ran his hands over her shoulders, her arms, under the hem of the shirt she wore. God, it made him so hot to see her in his shirt. He squeezed her behind and her thighs, nudging them open with his legs. When she went to lean in to him, he held her back against the desk and knelt down in front of her.

"Keith," she whispered as he pulled her panties down.

"Shhh," he said, and then his mouth was on her, making her crazy. He lifted one leg over his shoulder so he could taste deeper, and soon she was whimpering, then shaking as she came apart on his face. He caught her as her legs gave out and she collapsed on top of him on the floor.

"I can't believe we just did that on top of the invoices," she said into his neck.

He laughed and held her close.

Chapter 27

"No more of that rabbit food!"

Cal was participating in his new favorite activity: sitting on the couch and yelling at Mal and Miss Libby as they cooked in the kitchen. He had been out of the hospital for less than a day before he started going stir crazy, and it was just getting worse. The doctor ordered him to rest (impossible) and diet (unheard of).

"You can't teach this old dog new tricks," he pleaded.

"You can if you want to live to see your grandchildren," said Miss Libby.

Mal felt like everyone was looking at her and she blushed down to her toes. "I'm not pregnant."

Cal looked at her with a raised eyebrow. "Why would you be pregnant?"

Mal was really starting to embrace healthy food preparation. She visited the library, and the librarian helped her pick out a few diet cookbooks. She did it so often that the librarian even kept them aside for her for her regular visits. "No one else around here uses them. Have you been to the fair? That food on a stick is delicious!"

Mal's favorite was a low-fat vegetarian cookbook, which she had to hide in her bedroom. She would write down the recipes, then head to the kitchen to surreptitiously cook them. Even Miss Libby was concerned about a meal without meat; even patient Keith, who never complained about anything, was aghast.

"Where's your sense of adventure?" she asked, serving a fake-meat veggie casserole.

The Carsons may have been a lot of things, but they were not adventurous. They also, apparently, were not vegetarians. So now Mal hid the vegetarian nature of the meals she served (most of them, anyway), and figured they would thank her when their cholesterol lowered.

She was pleased to discover that there were a few things she could teach Libby in the kitchen. Libby was an expert at cooking with butter and shortening, but she genuinely seemed to appreciate the low-fat substitutes Mal showed her. Mal was not pleased that her knowledge came from Michael pressuring her into dieting with cruel comments, but, as Libby said, she should be grateful part of it turned out to be a blessing.

Miss Libby was looking for blessings everywhere. The Carson kids, such as they were, were shaken up by Cal's heart attack. True, they had faced the mortality of a parent before when their mom died of breast cancer all those years ago, but this was their father. Cal was always there, usually in the background, silently offering guidance. A force to keep from disappointing. He always made his presence known, in his way, and it was frightening to imagine him not being there.

But Miss Libby was taking it extra hard. She and Cal were at each other's throats all the time, and not in the playful, teasing way that Keith was used to seeing. He walked into the kitchen once to find Miss Libby crying quietly into the sink.

"I was a coward," Keith told Mal as they cuddled in bed that night. They had been spending the nights together since Cal came home. Libby pretended to be too busy to notice. "I just backed out of the kitchen like I hadn't seen her."

"Well, she probably would have been embarrassed. She doesn't want you to know how hard she's taking your father's illness."

"I feel bad, it's just more work for her."

Mal lifted her head off Keith's shoulder. "That's not it at all. She was terrified she would lose him."

Keith grunted, and stroked Mal's hair. He liked doing that; her hair was short and soft, and the stroking made her relax, which right now meant she was cuddling closer into his side. He definitely liked that.

"Keith."

"Mmm?"

"I think Miss Libby is in love with your father."

Keith shot up, knocking Mal aside. He absentmindedly grabbed her arms and held her to him. "That doesn't make any sense. My father is a miserable grump."

"OK, first of all, are you seriously expecting love to make sense?"

Keith grudgingly agreed. "But they argue all the time now."

"I think Cal likes her, too. They just can't admit it, so they take it out on each other. Like Katie and Chase do."

"Katie and Chase? Now I know you're being crazy. They hate each other."

Mal sighed and snuggled back into Keith's side. His arms automatically came around her.

"Anyway, your father is not a miserable grump. He's a little rough around the edges, maybe, but he has his charm."

Keith snorted. She was definitely crazy. He loved it.

Mal had been sleeping in the bunkhouse with Keith since she got back. At first she thought she shouldn't, she should continue to respect Miss Libby's house rules. But then Keith had come over, throwing rocks at her window again, sneaking her out of the house. In the morning, he snuck her back in. One morning Libby caught them kissing on the doorstep at dawn.

"You two might as well come in and help me with breakfast. Keith, put the coffee on. Mal, get in here, you're freezing!"

"Miss Libby, I'm sorry that—"

"Don't you mind that, you're a grown woman. Although I do appreciate you making the effort."

She and Keith were definitely a couple now. They spent time together, sorting out paperwork (her favorite) and making plans for Keith to get his vet certification back (Dr. Monroe's favorite). The whole family put in time on his old cottage, tearing down walls, painting. Keith didn't think he was ready to live there, but he hoped he and Mal would start looking for a place together soon. He couldn't expect her to live in a bunkhouse forever. Anyway, Katie seemed to be staking a claim on the cottage, so maybe that would force his hand. He was starting to get that itch to buy some property; he had been raised with the idea that a man needed his own land. Mal said she didn't care where they lived, and that he should focus on preparing to take over Dr. Monroe's practice. He figured they would get sick of each other then—she was still doing Dr. Monroe's books, so they would be working together all the time.

But even now, when they were working separately, they always sought each other out before too long. Mal tried not to compare it to her relationship with Michael (who still hadn't returned any of her calls). When she was with Michael, she never sought him out, and in fact, she spent as much time as possible avoiding him without looking like she was avoiding him. Their time together was strained and, even when they were young and at their best, she'd never felt as comfortable as she did with Keith.

Or as loved.

Keith told her he loved her every chance he got—when they ate together, when she fought with power tools, and especially when they made love. She would find herself stopping in the middle of cooking a meal, lost in the memory, blushing. She burned a whole pile of asparagus that way, much to Cal's delight.

Chapter 28

"I don't know why he's avoiding me," Mal said to Luke as they sat in the kitchen sipping coffee. "You'd think he would want to put this divorce through as fast as possible."

"Maybe he's dead," Luke said hopefully. They were taking a break from working on a budget for Luke's stud business. He was pretty eager for the distraction.

"It makes me nervous, that's all. Like he's cooking something up out there, and I'm going to be married to him forever."

"You know what? He probably loves having you chasing after him. Leave him alone for a few days, he'll come crawling back to you."

"Luke, I don't want to take that kind of risk. Michael can be so unpredictable, and the last few times I talked to him . . ."

"Honey, I know. I met him, remember? And maybe you're right, maybe he's coming unhinged and is cooking up some nefarious plan. But what you're doing now isn't working, so you might as well try another tactic. Let him think you don't care."

"Yeah."

"And, sweetheart, I don't think you should go to DC on your own."

"Luke—"

"Please, Mal. If for no other reason, then take someone with you for my peace of mind. You don't want me suffering, do you?"

Mal laughed. "I would never. Anyway, Keith said he would go with me."

Luke raised his eyebrows. "Keith agreed to go to a city? Darlin', it must be love."

Mal blushed. "Well, we're not going anywhere until I hear from

Michael. I hate not knowing what he's thinking." She sighed into her coffee. "Maybe he really is dead. Oh, that's a horrible thing to say!"

Luke laughed. "Maybe he's just injured in a ditch somewhere. Nonfatal. Oh, maybe he has amnesia! And he's in a coma! And when he wakes up, he'll be an actual human being!"

Mal laughed. "OK, enough procrastinating. Let's take another look at these figures."

"Ugh." Luke slumped in his chair. "I never thought I would dread looking at figures."

The next day, Katie came charging through the kitchen, looking for Luke. Mal had told her they were working on a business plan, and if Luke thought he was going to cut her out of it . . .

The ringing phone stopped her and she grabbed the receiver. "Hello!" she barked.

"Mallory?"

"No, who is this?"

"I'm looking for Mallory. My wife."

"Oh, you must be Michael. Wonderful. I've heard so much about you."

"Well, you're very charming in your hillbilly way, but I would like to speak to my wife."

"You mean ex-wife."

"She didn't tell you? She hasn't signed the divorce papers yet. I've been trying to get hold of her for weeks. She left me an address to send the papers to, but that doesn't sound very safe. I think she needs to come back here——"

"Listen, Michael." Katie was practically spitting, she was so mad. "I don't know what you think you're trying to pull, but Mal has friends here and we're not just going to let her——Hey!" She turned to face Chase, who had come up behind her and pushed the receiver down to hang up. "I wasn't done talking to him!"

Chase pried the receiver out of Katie's white-knuckled grip. "Pissing him off isn't going to help Mal any."

"Well! He's delusional if he thinks she'll just drop everything for him anymore! Somebody needs to set him straight!"

"But not you."

She looked at him, her eyes furious, her mouth set. "Fine," she said, storming out of the kitchen.

The night air was crisp, but the sky was clear and the moon was full and bright. Mal sat on the porch swing, wrapped in a few blankets to ward off the chill, absentmindedly counting stars. She couldn't get over how many more stars there seemed to be in Kentucky than in DC. The benefits of living in the middle of nowhere, she supposed.

"Hey." Keith climbed the steps, his big work boots making the boards creak.

"Hay is for horses," she said, smiling at him.

"Aren't you cold?"

"Yes. But it's too beautiful a night to sit inside. Come keep me warm," she said, scooting over on the swing to make room for him.

"Here," he said, handing her a bunch of flowers. In the bright moonlight, she could see the yellows and oranges and reds.

"What's that for?"

"The colors reminded me of the leaves. You were saying yesterday how sad it looked now that the leaves have all fallen. So, I thought——"

"That's very sweet. Thank you." She laughed and pulled him down to kiss him.

"Wait, um. I don't want to sit outside with you. And not just because it's freezing out here."

"Wimp."

"Come with me," he said, holding out his hand. She gathered her flowers, left the blankets, and let him lead her out into the night.

She wasn't surprised when he led her to the bunkhouse, or when he led her into his bedroom. What did surprise her were the candles everywhere, on the dresser, surrounding the bed. There were rose petals—actual wild rose petals!—on the bed. She looked up at him. He was holding her hand tightly. Was he nervous?

"I had to leave Peanut up at the house. I was afraid he would knock over the candles. I figured it wouldn't be very romantic if we had to use a fire extinguisher."

"It's beautiful," she said, looking around the room. Candlelight sparkled off the mirror, off the old brass of the bed.

"I wanted to do something special, you know? I know with

Michael, he could give you whatever you wanted. I just wanted to show you—"

She silenced him with a hand over his mouth. Not quite as gently as she meant to do it, but, well, it shut him up. "Michael gave me nothing that I wanted. You give me everything."

"Yeah, I give you a barn and hard labor and a cranky old man—"

"You give me your heart. That's all I want," she said, wrapping her arms around his neck.

"Oh," he said, letting her pull him forward, kissing him, kissing her back.

She led him to the bed; they slowly removed each other's clothes, gently exploring bodies, loving the curves, the scars, loving each other. She pulled him on top of her, spreading her legs for him. As he entered her, she exhaled in pure pleasure at the way he filled her so completely. They began to move, slow, loving movements that soon turned insistent, reaching. She looked into his eyes, her fingers tangled in his hair. "I love you," she whispered, and they came apart together.

Chapter 29

Mal woke up to the sound of Peanut's barking. It was still dark out, and she was warm, her limbs tangled with Keith's. She sighed and nestled closer: Peanut would sort it out, whatever it was.

Then she tensed as she heard someone swearing at Peanut. It was a voice she'd been waiting for, but hearing it now, outside the room where she slept, twisted her stomach. Michael. She climbed out of bed and hurried to the window, and there he was, raising his hand to Peanut, who thought he was playing a game, nipping at him playfully.

"Shit," she said, and began throwing on her clothes.

"What is it?" Keith asked sleepily from the bed.

"Nothing, I'll be back in a second."

"'Kay," he said, rolling over to his side and going back to sleep.

Mal shook her head, smiling, as she slipped on her boots and ran quietly down the stairs, and out to meet her soon-to-be-ex-husband.

He still had his hand raised to Peanut, who seemed to have figured out that this wasn't a game and was growling at him, crouching down, hackles raised.

"Michael!"

Michael didn't take his eyes off of Peanut. "Call off your damn dog."

"Peanut, come." Peanut trotted dutifully over to her, licked her hand, then took a protective stance in front of her.

Michael finally looked at her, surprised at the direction she'd come from. "Are you sleeping in the barn? And what the hell did you do to your hair?"

"Michael, what are you doing here?"

"I bet you can guess."

Mal didn't like the manic look she saw in his eyes. "You brought me the divorce papers to sign?" she asked, hopefully. Stupidly.

"No, Mallory. I told you I would track you down. I came to bring you home."

"Mal? You OK?" Keith was emerging from the bunkhouse, headed toward them. Peanut barked quietly, keeping his position in front of Mal.

"Who is this? Is this the other brother? The one you're screwing?"

"Michael!"

"You're my wife, dammit!"

She wasn't sure how she hadn't noticed it before, but she was sure she was the last one to do so. Peanut was growling protectively, and Keith had stopped several yards from them, his hands in the air. She looked at him, puzzled, then looked back at Michael, who was pointing a handgun in her face.

"Jesus, Michael!" Her heart stuttered in fear. How much more of this was she going to take from him? He wouldn't stop until she was dead. That thought fostered a kernel of indignation, a spark of anger that he would take her life just when she was starting to enjoy it. She held on to that anger as he waved his gun.

"I told you, I'm bringing you home! You're my wife!"

He reached for her, but Peanut growled and crouched lower.

"Call off that dog or I'll shoot him!"

She had never seen him quite like this. Even when he'd hit her, he was strangely calm. He had never looked out of control before. That, more than the gun, frightened her.

"Keith, call Peanut!"

"Mal!" His voice was gruff behind her. He sounded far away.

"Keith, please!"

She thought he wasn't going to do it, he waited that long. "Peanut, come here."

Peanut didn't look back at Keith, but his ears twitched.

"Again, Keith, please!"

He called the dog again. This time Peanut looked at Mal. "Go," she said, her voice firm. Peanut ran to Keith, sitting in front of him, facing Mal and Michael. "Good dog," she heard Keith say softly.

"Stupid dog," Michael said. "Is this what you do here? Sleep with the redneck brothers, take in cripples? Mallory, I can give you so much more. I *have* given you so much more. You've made your point, I didn't appreciate you. Now come home."

"Michael, please, just go. There's nothing for you here."

"My *wife* is here."

"You left me for Bunny Ashton-Pierce!" Stop provoking him, Mal! Michael faltered. "I am willing to admit an error in judgment. Now get in the car!"

She felt a movement behind her. "Don't move or I swear I'll shoot you!" Michael shouted. Keith. *Keith, don't be stupid,* she pleaded silently.

Keith was stupid, though, and he moved forward to try to get between Mal and Michael. Between Mal and Michael's gun. But Keith didn't know Michael like she did, didn't know that Michael was a lot of things, but he wasn't a faker and he didn't like his territory threatened. So she shouldn't have been surprised when the gun went off.

"No!" she said, diving for Keith. He went down; she tried to catch him, collapsing at his side. "Keith!"

"Mal, run. Please!" Keith's shirt was covered in blood; where was all that blood coming from?

"That's right, baby. You're back where you belong," Michael said, pulling her up and toward the car, keeping his gun trained on Keith. "There's no need to cry," he said, wiping her tears. She flinched, then flinched again when he kissed her. She kept her lips shut tight.

She heard a *click* and Cal's voice behind her. "Let go of the girl and get the hell off my property."

Michael laughed and started to reply, but Mal took advantage of the distraction and lifted her knee. Hard.

Michael doubled over in pain, clutching his groin, still holding the gun.

She turned and ran back to Keith, who was looking paler, bloodier.

Peanut streaked past her, teeth bared, looking like the ferocious beast she had mistaken him for the first time she saw him.

She turned back, kept running toward Keith. She was almost there, had almost reached him. She heard a shot go off and she stumbled, but she crawled the last few paces to Keith and shielded his body with hers, turning back to face the others. Through the haze of tears, she saw Peanut, his jaw attached to Michael's wrist, the gun abandoned on the ground. Cal had his rifle trained on Michael, was shouting to Libby to call the cops. Katie was running out of the house, a shotgun in her hand, the phone up to her ear. Mal blinked, turned down to Keith. "Hold on," she whispered.

He lifted his hand. It was covered in blood, but Mal grabbed it, brought his palm to her face. "Hold on, Keith. Please, hold on."

Chapter 30

Mal knew her way around a hospital, but she barely knew where she was now. The fog that had descended on her when they shut the ambulance doors hadn't lifted yet. Keith was in surgery. One of the nurses had brought her into an exam room, cleaned her up, checked her for injuries. *I'm fine*, she wanted to scream. *I'm not the one who was shot in the chest by my crazy husband!*

Now she sat in a hard plastic chair in the waiting room. Libby sat next to her, squeezing her hand, muttering comforting words she couldn't quite make out. Cal and Katie had stayed behind to talk to the police, but they were apparently on their way now. Libby wanted the doctors to check Cal's heart, which was enough for him to try to keep away. Great, Mal thought. They would all be there to see what she had done to Keith.

"Here we are again," Mal said.

"Yes. I hope not to make it a habit."

"Libby, I'm so sorry," she whispered.

"Hush now," Libby said, and wrapped her arm tightly around Mal.

"I brought this trouble here. It's my fault."

"Mal, I'm only going to say this once." Libby tilted Mal's chin so she was looking into her eyes. "This is not your fault. Everybody is responsible for their own actions. You did not drive Michael here. You did not point his gun at my boy." Her voice broke. "Do you hear me? This is not your fault."

"But—"

"No." She jerked Mal's chin. "And that's all I want to hear about that."

Mal looked at Libby, her chin quivering but her eyes determined.

How had Mal been so lucky to find these people? How could she lose them now?

The doctor came out, pulling the paper wrapper off his head. Libby jumped up to greet him. Mal couldn't move. She saw him lower his head and speak quietly to Libby, saw Libby buckle and shout, "Oh, thank the Lord," and Mal was on her feet.

"Is he OK? Can I see him?"

"He was lucky. The bullet missed his heart and went clean through. He's going to have a rough road ahead of him, but he is out of danger."

"Can I see him?"

"He's still unconscious, but you can go in if you're quiet."

"Go on, Mal. He'll need to see you when he wakes up."

There were so many tubes. And the beeping. After two days, though, Mal found the beeping comforting. It meant everything was working, that Keith was healing. He had woken up a few times, groggy and a little cranky. She took that to be a good sign—he was so much like his father, surely crankiness was a sign of recovery? All of the Carsons had been in to see him, and Libby brought her food that she barely touched. Mal hadn't left his side, except for last night when Luke dragged her home to shower ("You stink, woman. Let Keith wake up to something beautiful, OK?"), and to sleep. She was back at dawn, listening to the beeping, stroking Keith's forehead.

Her back was starting to cramp. She got up to pace around the room. The view out the window was not as distracting as she hoped it would be—just the roof of the next building. Not even a parking lot—some good people watching would have been nice. She stretched her arms above her head and leaned down to touch her toes.

"Hey."

She stood up too fast and knocked into the bedside tray.

"You OK?"

Mal let out the breath she was holding. "You're recovering from a gunshot wound and you're asking if I'm OK?"

Keith squinted. "What?"

The doctor had told Mal that Keith might not remember everything about the other night. She approached the bed quietly.

"Keith, you were shot. Michael shot you."

"Is that why my chest hurts?"

"Yes."

He sighed. "I thought you might break my heart. This isn't what I had in mind."

And that was it. Mal couldn't stop the tears from pouring down her cheeks.

"Hey, hey, don't cry. That was a joke."

"I know. It was a good one."

Keith raised his eyebrows weakly.

"Keith, I'm so sorry."

"Come here."

Mal stepped closer to the bed and picked up his hand.

"No, come here." He tugged her down until she was sitting on the edge of the bed. He tugged her again so she was lying down next to him.

"Stop, I don't want to hurt you."

"I'm sick, humor me."

He grunted as he moved over, making room for her. He put his arm around her and pulled her close.

"Be careful."

"Hush," he said, kissing her forehead.

She lay there for a minute, soaking in his smell. Hospital and Keith.

"Does it hurt?"

Keith snorted. "Like hell."

"Oh, Keith."

"Michael shot me?"

"Yes."

"Did you shoot him back?"

Mal's laugh was a little watery. "No. But Cal and Katie were ready to."

"Nobody shot him?"

"Didn't have to. Peanut tackled him."

"I knew that was a good dog."

She raised her hand and pushed his hair off his forehead. "Do you need anything? Ice? More pain medicine?"

"I just need to hold you and be quiet."

"OK."

"Keep doing that, though. I have a killer headache."

"You're probably dehydrated."

"Quiet, remember?"

She ran her fingers through his hair, gently running them over his forehead, his cheeks, his chin. She ran her hand gently around the bandage on his chest.

She tried to be quiet. She really did. But the tears kept running down her face, wetting his sterile hospital sheets. "So close to your heart," she whispered.

Keith didn't say anything, just took her hand, placed a gentle kiss on her palm, then on the inside of her wrist. He tugged her arm so she leaned closer to him, and traced the tears down her cheek. He pulled her closer.

Mal found she couldn't cry when Keith was kissing her.

Chapter 31

Keith was released from the hospital a few days later. He joined Cal, unhappily convalescing in the living room. Keith didn't have enough energy to really complain, though, and Cal seemed a little more subdued after he gave up the couch for his son.

Gradually, eventually, life at the Wild Rose moved on.

As winter deepened, Mal got to work. She negotiated some new billing software for Dr. Monroe's office, she squirreled away her money and bought an old compact car, and she tried to get Luke to teach her what was so great about studs.

"Money makers, Mal. People around here will kill for this guy's services," he said, patting the rump of the not-quite-Triple-Crown winner he'd gotten for a bargain at auction.

"There's a lot we have to set up, man," Chase said, rubbing his eyes. Katie was banned from the room because she couldn't stop arguing with everything Luke said. Not that she was wrong, but Chase had a much more productive way of handling it. So Chase and Mal and Luke sat around the dining room table, discussing investment partners and business names that did not involve the word "stallion."

Mal had tried to get Cal interested, not so much in Luke's side project ("waste of time," as Cal called it), but at least in bringing Wild Rose into the twenty-first century. She finally got him to agree that a simple logo would not be too "fancy-ass," and somehow she managed to get him interested in a Web site. She was working with Libby on the history of some of the older buildings on the farm, and went to the library a few times to scan old photos to include on the site. It wasn't the most mind-blowing Web site she had ever seen, but it was functional and informative. Sort of a metaphor for the Wild Rose.

And Michael finally granted her the divorce. His arguments against it were less than persuasive, making them as he did from behind prison walls. He was charged with attempted murder and carrying a weapon without a permit, and the prosecutor got some stalking and harassment thrown in there for good measure. There was even talk that Mal would get some of his money when his assets were unfrozen. She wasn't sure she wanted it. She would give it all to the Carsons if they would take it, but as it was, she had to sneak out to the grocery store to be able to pitch in at all. The further she got from her marriage to Michael, though, the more she saw what it had cost her. She *had* earned that money. And there was definitely a battered women's shelter somewhere that could use it.

And then there was Keith. He was making a slow recovery, but she did her best to cook him healing foods and make him comfortable and keep him out of the stables. He, like Cal, was not great at sitting still. She finally got her wish and was able to tackle the Wild Rose office, filing with an unprecedented fury. She took over some of the bookkeeping responsibilities, but made sure Katie had the lion's share. Cal seemed dead set against Katie taking over, but since he didn't want to hire a business manager while Keith recovered, he reluctantly agreed. Of course, Keith had no intention of returning to Wild Rose—Dr. Monroe had been by several times to talk about Keith coming back to the practice.

Mal had spent so much of her life feeling unsure about everything that it was a little unsettling to feel that something was so right. But it was. She knew in her heart Keith was the man for her, and that his family was her family.

Keith was going nuts. On the one hand, he loved seeing Mal become part of his family. She had kept those smarts of hers hidden, but she really had a head for business. And she was a cool negotiator, getting Cal to agree to things he would never have imagined—a Web site, for Pete's sake. She mediated arguments between Katie and Luke, Katie and Chase, Katie and Cal. In fact, Katie seemed to really respect Mal, a right not easily won.

But he was going crazy. Because while Mal was out making her mark on Wild Rose, he was laid up in bed. Oh, sure, she came to see him several times a day, checked his bandage, mopped his forehead. But as the haze of pain wore off and he moved back into his own house, his frustration level rose. She wouldn't kiss him, not properly. She wouldn't stay the night—even just to sleep, he promised. He thought he saw the same love in her eyes that he had seen before, but, dammit, she was spending more time with his family than she was with him.

That was going to change.

He bribed Luke into saddling Blue for him. The night was freezing, and a few flakes of snow were starting to fall. Mal had told him she loved how the hills looked with a dusting of snow. This was probably the last snow of the winter, her last chance to enjoy it. *All for love,* he thought, as he hoisted himself up on Blue. He winced at the pain, but once he was up there, he was fine. Blue could pretty much walk herself, so he gently guided her out of the stable and toward the house.

It was snowing again. Mal was still not quite used to these teaser snows, where flakes would fall for hours, but none of them would stick. Still, she loved watching the snow fall against the backdrop of the dark night sky. She rested her elbows on the windowsill and her head on the glass. She wrapped Keith's shirt tighter around her. How pathetic, sleeping in her man's shirt. But that was the closest she could get to him, at least while he was still recovering.

She jumped back at a sudden *tap* on the window. She flinched at another, then another. When she looked down, there was Keith, bundled in his hat and blankets, riding Blue.

"Are you crazy?" she whispered, throwing the window open. "You're going to kill yourself!"

"I'm fine! Come down!"

"It's freezing!"

"Then get your coat! Come down here, Mal."

"No!"

"I'm staying out here until you do."

"Keith!"

"How much of this do you think I can stand, in my fragile state?"

She hoped he could see her disapproving glare from where he

was. But, in the end, she grabbed her coat and her boots and met him outside.

"You're going to have to hoist yourself up here," Keith said, reaching out his hand.

"I'm not getting up there! I'll kill you!"

"What are you going to do, walk next to me?"

She glared again, but put her foot on top of his and pulled herself up.

"You're getting good at that," he grunted as her back collided with his chest.

"Sorry!"

"Hush," he said, wrapping the blanket around her. He kicked Blue and they rode off.

"Where are we going?"

"Just for a ride," he said, leaning in to kiss her neck.

"In the snow?"

"It'll stop in a minute."

She sighed and leaned against him. "Oh! Does that hurt?"

"No. Come closer," he said, holding her against him.

They rode in silence, his arms around her waist, her head resting on his shoulder. He took her on the path they rode that first time together, then through a clearing where the moon shone so bright it was almost daylight. Blue kept a gentle pace, and soon Keith felt Mal get heavy.

"Hey," he said, nudging her gently. "Are you falling asleep?"

"No," she said drowsily. "Where are we going?"

"Just for a ride, I told you."

"You couldn't wait for spring?"

"I might not be here in the spring."

"What?" She turned as much as she could, trying to see his face. "Where are you going?"

"Not far." He laughed, tucking her hat back into place. "I put in an offer on some land up the road."

"The one we looked at the other day?"

"Yup."

"The one with the little cottage that's falling down?"

"Yes. That will need some work."

"I love that cottage."

"I know. I love that land."

"So you're moving?"

"That's the idea. It's a lot for one person, though."

"Yeah?"

"Yeah."

He just smiled that crooked smile and kissed her neck and her cheek until she twisted farther and then he kissed her mouth. It had been so long since he'd tasted her. He grunted in pleasure, and cupped her cheek, opening her mouth with his tongue, deepening the kiss.

"Wait, hold on," she said, breathless.

"I can't wait," he said, leaning back down to her.

"Be careful," she said, placing her hand gently on his chest.

He ignored her and pulled her close for another kiss. Soon they were both panting and she was twisting in the saddle, trying to get closer.

"Are we going to have sex on the horse?" she asked, her eyes sparkling.

Keith laughed, breathless, and rested his forehead on hers. "I don't think Blue would like that very much."

Mal turned ahead and rested her head against his shoulder again. She leaned back to brush a kiss on his neck. "Take me home," she whispered.

So he did.

Mal didn't want to go to sleep. She wanted to stay awake and remember this night forever. But Keith was so warm, and his arms felt so strong around her. The fire was crackling, and, frankly, she was exhausted. Even though she'd been gentle with Keith, he'd still managed to wear her out. She sighed and burrowed deeper under the blankets.

"You don't want to move to the bed?" he asked, stroking her back. They were piled on cushions on the floor in front of the couch, which, for all their gentleness, was as far as they could make it. Afterward, Mal had grabbed as many blankets as she could find and wrapped them up, and let Peanut in the house, too, since he was making an unholy ruckus being excluded from the warmth. And attention.

"No. It's too cozy here. And I can't move."

He laughed softly, kissed the top of her head.

"You know, I thought you were going to ask me to marry you tonight," Mal said, looking at the fire. When he didn't say anything, she continued, "The way you seemed to make a big deal out of getting me up on the horse and going out in the snow, and then talking about the land and the house."

He squeezed her shoulder, but kept silent.

"And then I thought, as we were riding, that you were going to pull a ring out from under a rock or something."

She felt him swallow. Hard.

"And I almost didn't come down," Mal continued. "I almost risked you breaking the window again so I could stay up there. Because the idea of you asking me to marry you and me having to say no, it just, I just couldn't take it."

She turned to look at him, bending her right knee so it was leaning on his hip. He automatically wrapped his arm around her leg, but continued to stare into the fire.

"And then I thought, why the hell would I say no? Here is a man who respects me, who understands me, who *loves* me for me, which is what I've always wanted and what I never thought I could have, not after—well, I just didn't think that kind of man existed, the kind of man who would match me like that. But it's you. You match me, because I love you as much as you love me, and I love everything about you. I love how you're willing to admit your mistakes, how you fight for hopeless cases, how you've opened your heart to me. Your whole family took me in, and for that I'll be forever grateful. But it's you I'm most grateful for, it's you I love the best."

Without looking at her, Keith got up and paced in front of the fire, wrapping one of the smaller blankets around his waist.

Mal took a deep breath. "So, OK. So why would I say no? There's no reason. I had a bad marriage before, but that's the past, that's not you. So I was ready to say yes."

Keith stiffened, but he kept pacing.

Mal cleared her throat. "But then, well, you didn't ask. But you know what? I've spent my entire adult life doing what other people tell me to do, acting like they think I'm supposed to act. And I'm sick of it. Dammit, Keith, I love you, and I want to marry you!"

Keith finally stopped. "What?"

"I want to marry you." She sat up on her knees, the blankets pooled around her waist, her skin glowing in the firelight. "What I mean is, will you marry me?"

"What?" he said, blinking stupidly.

"Well, if you're not going to ask me, why shouldn't I ask you?" She was seriously losing confidence here. "I just thought—"

He left the room.

Mal stared after him for a second, blinking the hurt from her eyes. She turned back toward the fire, and pulled the blankets tight around her shoulders. *That went well,* she thought.

She was just starting to get up the energy to pull on her clothes when Keith came back.

"Wha—" she said, as he dropped down in front of her with a small box in his hand.

"I didn't want to interrupt your pretty speech," Keith said, taking the ring out and holding it up to her. "And I'm glad I didn't. It kind of had the ending I was looking for."

Mal looked at the ring he was holding, blinking back tears. It was beautiful, white gold with a small amber stone surrounded by tiny diamonds.

"I know it's not the usual, but, I don't know, I thought it matched your eyes."

"Yes," she said.

"I haven't even asked yet," Keith said, laughing.

"I already asked. So it's your turn to answer."

"Yes," Keith said, slipping the ring on her finger. "Yes, I will marry you." And this time when he pulled her onto his lap she didn't complain. She just kissed him.

Peanut lifted his head. His human pillow was jostling him too much for him to get any rest. There they were again, all over each other. Like animals. He stood up, stretched his one front leg and two hind, curled up in front of the fire, and went to sleep.

Epilogue

It was a late-summer wedding. They wanted to wait for the mud from the wet winter to dry up, and that gave them more time to put a fresh coat of paint on the barn and fix up the yard. It wasn't a huge wedding, although you wouldn't have known from the amount of food Libby made. Mal tried to help her as much as possible, but every time Libby looked at her, she broke out in happy tears, so Mal decided it would be better if she just left her to fend for herself.

"Who's going to walk you down the aisle?" Luke asked.

She had thought about asking him to do it, since he had, however inadvertently, brought her and Keith together. But he was standing up as Keith's best man, and she didn't want to upset the delicate truce between the brothers.

Katie thought she should walk herself down the aisle. "You're your own woman. No man should give you away."

They were getting married at the house, the ceremony officiated by Billie, who got her certification on the Internet. It wasn't the most traditional way to start a life together, but that seemed to be par for the course for them. Besides, Billie loved them both and she was thrilled to get the chance to wear something other than scrubs.

Jack was with Mal in the upstairs bathroom, "trying to do something with this hair." It had grown to about her chin since he'd cut it last, and it was a frizzy mess in the humidity. "Just make it look like me," she told him. Jack was smoothing it out, finagling it to fall naturally around her face, assuring her that he had been over in the bunkhouse and that Keith's hair was combed and he had shaved.

They were so informal as a couple that they'd decided to get married in a casual ceremony—sundresses for the women, no ties for the men. Mal was wearing a calf-length sheath that Libby had helped her make. Well, she'd pinned the pieces together; Libby did everything else. It was cut against the bias, with seams that ran at a diagonal around her body and a low scoop neck. It was sleeveless, so she wore an antique lace wrap that had been Libby's mother's.

"Something borrowed, sweetheart."

Jack approved, which was good. He said it "hugged her curves, but not in a slutty way."

Luke came into the kitchen once when they were doing a fitting, dropping a sledgehammer on his foot.

"He likes it," Katie had said.

In the bunkhouse, Keith was getting ready by himself, which suited him fine. Jack had checked to make sure he was going to tuck in his shirt, then made a joke about plucking his eyebrows. At least Keith thought it was a joke.

He hadn't gotten much sleep last night. Libby had insisted that Mal spend the night in the house, not in the bunkhouse with Keith. "At least give an old woman the pretense of innocence," she said. It was more than a pretense, though, since when Keith tried to sneak in the back door to secret his bride-to-be away, he found it locked and the key was not in its usual place under the rock.

So he made his way over to the side of the house, picking up a pocketful of pebbles along the way. He started to throw them at Mal's window, only stopping when he saw the reading light come on. Her hand shot out of the open window. "OK! OK, I see you! Don't throw anything, please."

She poked her head out and his heart stopped. She was beautiful in the faint glow of the reading lamp and the moon from above. She was wearing an old T-shirt—one of his, from a football camp he went to in high school—and her hair was sticking out in strange waves from sleep.

"Hey, beautiful," he whispered. "Want to go for a walk?"

She smiled, then darted from the window. A few minutes later he caught her up in his arms as she raced out of the house.

They walked toward the orchard for a while, holding hands. "Hey, what are you doing tomorrow?" Mal asked.

"Oh, I don't know, I thought I'd go squirrel hunting." She knocked him with her hip, and he feigned injury and went down to the ground, dragging her with him.

"Hey! Don't get me all dirty!"

"What, you're not going to shower before the wedding?"

"Of course I am, but what is Miss Libby going to say when I wake up with dirt smudges on my face?"

"She's going to say that you look like a woman in love," he said, kissing her.

They both stopped at the sound of a breaking twig beyond them. Mal stiffened, and Keith strained his neck to look toward the noise, pushing her up and behind him. He squinted into the darkness. "Is that my father running around the yard naked?" He took a breath to holler at him, crazy old man, but Mal grabbed his arm. She pointed into the darkness, to the place Cal had just come from. Miss Libby, wrapped in a quilt, was skulking back to the house.

Keith turned to Mal, his face serious. "Please, if you love me at all, you will pretend we did not just see that."

She wrapped her arms around his neck, kissing him sweetly. "See what?"

Mal could barely look at Libby today, which was good because the older woman's crying was going to set her off, too. Jack declared her fabulous and escorted her down to the foyer. She was going to exit from the house, then walk up a makeshift aisle to where Keith would be waiting for her. Keith. Her Keith.

"Hey, you clean up pretty good," Katie said, tucking a curl behind her ear.

"No! Stop touching your hair, Katie! That piece is supposed to be in front!" Jack was having an apoplexy.

"Thanks, you look pretty good yourself," laughed Mal. Not many blondes could pull off a yellow dress, but Katie looked smashing in the strapless sundress they had picked out together.

"Ready?"

"Where's my guy?" Mal asked.

Jack sighed. "You're really doing this, aren't you?"

Mal smiled. "Yes, I'm really doing it. Besides, you wouldn't want all of your hard work to go to waste."

"I have got to get out of this town. A stylist of my talent reduced to being a lowly dog groomer for the day. I have drool on my shoes, you know. You're lucky I love you," he said, pecking Mal on the cheek. "And you, too, gorgeous," he said, kissing Katie, who huffed disbelievingly in response. Jack took his seat next to Trevor and the music started, as traditional as a bluegrass wedding band could sound. Luke and Chase were standing up with Keith, and Mal could swear she saw Chase wink at Katie.

Then the wedding march started and she took her first step down the aisle. Peanut, good, obedient dog that he was, walked proudly next to her on his three legs. He was brushed and groomed and his long fur was shining, and he actually looked handsome, which was a surprise to everyone but Mal. She knew there was a prince in there. True, he had eaten off the bow tie they tried to get him to wear, but it was a casual wedding, so nobody really cared.

When they reached the end of the aisle, Mal couldn't take her eyes off Keith. Jack was right, he had brushed his hair, but the wind had blown it out of place. He looked tousled and rugged. Perfect.

Peanut stopped directly in front of Mal, looking Keith straight in the eye. A few people in the audience laughed nervously—it didn't look like Peanut was going to let the ceremony go on. Then Peanut looked back at Mal, then up at Keith. He seemed to nod before trotting off to roll around in the dirt behind the wedding party.

Mal laughed, watching him. Then she felt Keith take her hand, warm and sure. "Ready?" he asked her.

She nodded. Billie raised her hands over their heads. "Dearly beloved . . ."

Can't wait to get back to Hollow Bend?
Here's a taste of *Kentucky Christmas*, available this November.

Andrew Bateman hated snow.

He was batting a thousand on this trip, really. He hated snow, he hated driving, and he hated selling people stuff they probably didn't need. He especially hated sales. But if his cousin hadn't given him this job, he'd be living with his mother. Once a man passes thirty, he doesn't like the idea of moving back in with his mother.

That was another thing he hated. Being thirty-one. Thirty was not so bad. Thirty-one seemed like: no turning back now, buddy. And what was he doing with his life? Well, aside from being Midwest Regional Sales Rep for Bateman Veterinary Supply, and kind of sucking at that. He had made about three sales in Indiana. Now he was just hoping for his next appointment to go well so he could go back to his dinky apartment above his cousin's garage and watch everyone sing holiday songs and drink cocoa and get fat.

He looked quickly at his smartphone. No reception. Dammit. His cousin had warned him about two things: one, that in Kentucky horse country, veterinary supplies were big money, and if they wanted to break into the market, they would have to start small; and two, don't get lost on any dirt roads. It was late, and he was beginning to feel lost as soon as he pulled off the interstate. He thought he would just find a place to stay, then call on . . . whoever it was early in the morning, then start the long drive back.

But when he pulled off the interstate, there were no hotels. No restaurants, not even street lights. He was beginning to think his cousin was playing one of his practical jokes, the kind that made Ed laugh and made Andrew end up with his pants around his ankles or stone-drunk in a biker bar. Kentucky wasn't even in the Midwest. He tapped his GPS, and it sputtered a direction at him. It had only worked sporadically since he crossed the border. Maybe he was just imagining that. Southern Indiana was pretty hilly; surely he'd had reception problems there, too. All he knew was that the satellite wouldn't pick up the signal unless he tapped the GPS. He was used to electronic equipment behaving when he asked it to, but this was getting ridiculous. He would have just turned it off and followed signs to—what was the town called? Hollow Bend, said the nice lady on the GPS. But there were no signs. Only darkness, and hills, and snow.

Billie Monroe loved snow.

She loved that feeling of putting on your snow boots and zipping your coat up to your chin and seeing your breath as you walked everywhere because it was too dangerous to drive. Besides, it hardly ever snowed in Hollow Bend, at least not enough to stick, and never this early in the winter. She was going to enjoy it.

She tried her best to skip as she approached the entrance to the Cold Spot, Hollow Bend's answer to a hipster hangout. Of course, there were no hipsters in Hollow Bend, so the Cold Spot adjusted accordingly. Everyone was happier with a honky-tonk anyway.

Her best friend, Katie Carson, was standing outside, shivering without her coat and talking to Trevor Blank, who was smoking a cigarette. And shivering. Billie rolled her eyes. Those two were doing their dance again. She had gone out with Trevor once or twice—every girl in town had—but found him a little . . . dumb. *That's not very nice*, she thought. But man, it was true. All those beautiful farm muscles and she still couldn't work up much enthusiasm. It was hard to get too excited over a guy who thought Shakespeare was a fancy mixed drink.

Billie called out and Katie nodded in greeting, keeping her hands under her arms. But her face lit up in a big smile.

"Nice hat, Monroe," she said.

"You don't like it?" Billie said, fingering the red pom-pom bouncing on her head. "You're just jealous because Miss Libby made a hat for me and not for you."

"Oh, she made me a hat," said Katie, smiling. "I just conveniently lost it in the woods. In eighth grade."

"I like it," offered Trevor with a shrug. So cute, thought Billie. So cute and so, so dumb.

"Thank you, Trevor."

He smiled at her. Not happening, thought Billie. You better stake your claim on Katie before Chase gets here.

"Where's my brother?" Katie asked, stomping from one foot to the other. "I thought you said he was coming."

"Ugh, he's staying home," said Billie. "Today is the two-month anniversary of his coming back to work with my dad. But he said we celebrated enough for the one-month anniversary."

"And he wanted to get home to his pregnant wife?"

"He told you?" Billie asked. She had figured it out for herself. Mal had been sick every morning for a month but was still walking around with moony eyes. Keith was much worse, twice as moony as Mal, and every time she passed him, he would put his hands over her belly. For a man who barely spoke, Keith Carson was terrible at keeping secrets.

"No. We all figured it out when they came over for dinner last week. He wouldn't let Mal lift anything and every time he stood next to her, he put his hand over her belly. Miss Libby hasn't stopped crying."

"Yeah, when he came into the office last week, he couldn't stop smiling, even when he had to pull half a dish towel and a wristwatch out of the Coopers' dachshund."

"Well, I guess we're drinking alone," said Katie, opening the door.

"I'll keep you ladies company," said Trevor, following her inside.

Billie shook her head. She should be annoyed that her impromptu celebration was turning into a third-wheel night, but she couldn't muster up any irritation. She had been a good girl all autumn, and she wanted to cut loose. Besides, she had a lot to celebrate. Thanks to Keith, her father was finally getting ready to retire, it was a week before Christmas, and the night was young. She was about to get drunk with her best friend and a very handsome, if dumb, guy, and it was snowing—really snowing. That never happened in December. Nothing was going to ruin her night.

Until a car skidded on the street in front of her and crashed into the side of the bar.

* * *

One minute Andrew was shaking the GPS, because surely *this* was not the town his cousin had booked his sales call in. It hardly seemed big enough for a dog crate, let alone a vet practice. And the next his life was flashing before his eyes as he felt the back wheels lose traction and spin out. It was a short flash, which surprised him because he felt like this drive had aged him about seventy years. There were the plastic fire helmet, the Big Wheels, his first Mohawk, his mom making him grow out his first Mohawk, his first girlfriend, his first girlfriend dumping him, graduation, cubicle, cubicle, cubicle, pink slip. The car finally skidded to a stop with the help of a very sturdy-looking brick building that had no windows. The first thought Andrew registered, as his head snapped in slow-motion toward the air bag, was that he hoped the equipment samples in the trunk were okay or his cousin was going to kill him.

He let his head hit the air bag. What was the point?

Then everything came into sharp focus: his engine steaming, his shoulder burning under the locked seat belt, his head throbbing. Everything felt broken. If he died because of a sales call in Kentucky, he was going to kill his cousin.

A teenager with psychotic-anime eyes was pounding on his window. Oh, please, he thought, don't let me die here. Not until I get to kill my cousin. He focused on her face, every part of his body taking forever to respond to his command to MOVE.

She seemed to be shouting at him. He looked at her lips, and was startled that they were very pretty. No, he thought. He was not falling into this trap. If he went with her, he'd be dead and then he wouldn't be able to kill his cousin. But even through the foggy window and his haze of pain, he could see they were nice lips. He wondered if she would let him kiss her?

"Okay, okay," he read on her lips. Whoa, he thought. Kentucky was a nice place to die.

CPSIA information can be obtained at www.ICGtesting.com
Printed in the USA
BVOW08s2349230114

342838BV00001BA/72/P